The Christmas Project

The Royal Kensington Hospital's jet-set Christmas!

It's no secret that Christmas is the most wonderful time of the year! But for four of the Royal Kensington Hospital's top medical staff, this festive season will be one for the books… Why? They've just been invited to take part in the London hospital's prestigious Kensington Project!

With their passports in hand, the Royal Kensington Hospital's best and brightest are ready to share their specialist expertise—and the holiday season!—with hospitals around the world. From Jamaica to New York, and Toronto to Sweden, they're prepared to face busy wards and heart-racing emergencies. But a pulse-racing encounter or two under the mistletoe? No one included that in the Kensington Project's handbook! The expert team may be giving the gift of the Kensington Project this year…but will they receive the greatest gift of all—happily-ever-after?

Christmas Miracle in Jamaica by Ann McIntosh
December Reunion in Central Park by Deanne Anders
Available now!

Winter Nights with the Single Dad by Allie Kincheloe
Festive Fling in Stockholm by Scarlet Wilson
Coming soon!

Dear Reader,

Christmas in Jamaica!

I envy heroine Chloe Bailey for traveling to my homeland as part of the Kensington Project and being there for the holiday season. Jamaicans love to party, and in December you can do so every night, if you want.

But my most treasured Christmastime memories aren't of parties, but of trips to the country to see family; euphorbias and poinsettias blooming in the garden; Christmas puddings that are drunken, rum-soaked versions of their English ancestors; and drinking ruby-red sorrel. Of looking up into the clear blue sky and feeling the "Christmas breeze" blow cool across my skin, and singing old holiday songs that even now take me back to Grandma's house.

Chloe hopes to enjoy all the fun that is a Jamaican Christmas, but she's really there to share the expertise she's gained working at the Royal Kensington Hospital. Unbeknownst to her, there are life-changing surprises awaiting on the island—including surgeon Sam Powell, the man she never thought she'd see again, and a miraculous, precious gift.

I hope you'll enjoy Sam and Chloe's romance, which is seasoned with a *toops* (taste) of the joy and family that is the true spirit of Jamaica at Christmas.

Ann McIntosh

CHRISTMAS MIRACLE IN JAMAICA

———

ANN McINTOSH

HARLEQUIN

MEDICAL
ROMANCE

Special thanks and acknowledgment are given to Ann McIntosh for her contribution to The Christmas Project miniseries.

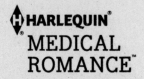

HARLEQUIN®
MEDICAL
ROMANCE™

Recycling programs for this product may not exist in your area.

ISBN-13: 978-1-335-40887-7

Christmas Miracle in Jamaica

Copyright © 2021 by Harlequin Books S.A.

For questions and comments about the quality of this book, please contact us at CustomerService@Harlequin.com.

Harlequin Enterprises ULC
22 Adelaide St. West, 40th Floor
Toronto, Ontario M5H 4E3, Canada
www.Harlequin.com

Printed in U.S.A.

Ann McIntosh was born in the tropics, lived in the frozen north for a number of years and now resides in sunny central Florida with her husband. She's a proud mama to three grown children, loves tea, crafting, animals (except reptiles!), bacon and the ocean. She believes in the power of romance to heal, inspire and provide hope in our complex world.

Books by Ann McIntosh

Harlequin Medical Romance

A Summer in São Paulo

Awakened by Her Brooding Brazilian

The Nurse's Pregnancy Miracle
The Surgeon's One Night to Forever
Surgeon Prince, Cinderella Bride
The Nurse's Christmas Temptation
Best Friend to Doctor Right
Christmas with Her Lost-and-Found Lover
Night Shifts with the Miami Doc
Island Fling with the Surgeon

Visit the Author Profile page at Harlequin.com.

For my sister, Kathy. Fruit is soaking, and this year we're making Christmas pudding together!

PROLOGUE

IT'S A NEW BEGINNING.

Seated at the end of the hotel bar, her shoulder against the wall, Chloe Bailey took a sip of tonic water and considered the thought carefully. Beyond the plate-glass window rain fell steadily, the gloomy San Francisco evening mirroring her mood.

Shouldn't she feel happy about the dawn of this next part of her life, especially after the horrid couple of years preceding it?

Perhaps she should, but instead of sparking joy, the rumination echoed morosely in her head, reminding her that success hadn't created this change. Failure had.

She wasn't used to failing. Actually, she'd lived her entire life conscientiously trying to avoid doing so.

Coloring within the lines.

Always doing what was expected.

Working hard to be the best.

Only taking considered risks so as not to make big mistakes.

Living what others erroneously thought was the perfect life.

It hadn't always been easy. Often she'd wished she didn't have the reputation for being reliable, steady, dependable. Especially when her parents used her as an example her siblings would do well to emulate, which had led to resentment when they were all younger and created an unrealistic vision of who she really was. And now...

She groaned quietly, and reached for her glass. Waves of hurt and embarrassment made her skin burn even as a shiver ran along her spine.

No one in her family had ever gotten divorced, until now.

Waking up five thousand miles away from her London home to her solicitor's text saying the entire ordeal of getting free from Finn was over had made her equal parts sad and relieved. Finn had fought the divorce every step of the way, making what should have been a straightforward matter into a circus. Creating discord, spouting ridiculous demands and accusations, trying to force Chloe to go back to him rather than go through with severing the marriage.

The mess he'd caused even had her parents questioning her decision. And just like that, Chloe was no longer the "perfect" daughter, sister or friend but someone others looked at with pity. Or speculation, since there were few people she entrusted with the true reason for the breakup, and Finn was almost universally liked.

It was all highly unfair, and as she drained the last of her sparkling water, Chloe couldn't help feeling resentful.

She hadn't cheated or lied. Finn had. Yet here she was, left holding the bag.

As she twisted the empty glass back and forth between her fingers, she heard her grandmother's voice, clear as day, as though the older lady was beside her and whispered into her ear.

"Anyone who thinks life is always going to be easy is a jackass. When things get tough, lift up your head and look for the advantage. There's always one, but usually you have to seek it out."

That was Gran's reaction anytime one of the family was dispirited or gloomy, but the familiar refrain rang hollow now.

"What possible advantage could there be to this mess?" she muttered.

But her brain was already whirring, putting aside the depressing, self-pitying thoughts and searching for the elusive silver lining.

Professionally, the breakup hadn't changed anything. Her position at the Royal Kensington Hospital was both secure and rewarding, and the cutting-edge research she was involved in gave her a great deal of satisfaction.

It was personally that she'd suffered, and perhaps that was where she could benefit?

All her life she'd been so careful, terrified of diminishing her good name, constantly aware that her parents expected her to set the best possible example for her younger siblings. Well, much of that had gone out the window over the last couple of years, leaving her...

Free.

To do things she'd wanted to but shied away from because they were risky or could potentially make others think less of her.

She'd always been so careful, so conservative and conventional. Wasn't it time she let loose a little?

"Can I get you another tonic water?"

Startled, Chloe looked up at the bartender, and instinctively nodded. "Yes, thank you."

She wasn't ready to retire to her lonely hotel bed, knowing she'd only lie sleepless while she wrestled with all the ramifications of the life-changes she was going through.

But as the other woman began to turn away, Chloe was struck by a totally different type of impulse.

"Wait," she said, causing the bartender to pause. "Do you serve mojitos?"

"Sure," the woman replied with a smile. "Wouldn't be a real bar if we didn't."

"I've always wanted to try one," Chloe said,

ignoring the whisper in her head telling her she rarely drank and she should be more careful, here in a strange city with no one to watch out for her.

"One mojito, coming up," the bartender said, her smile widening.

"Brilliant," Chloe replied, grinning in return.

When her drink came, she silently toasted her grandmother and her own quiet revolution, determined to make up for all the lost years of being so timid she'd forgotten how to actually *live*.

And when she found her gaze snagged by that of a very handsome man sitting across the bar, she refused to give in to the impulse to look away. Instead, she kept her eyes locked on his and raised her glass once more to her lips to sip the delicious liquid.

Then, as the gentleman in question rose and began to make his way toward her, she let herself smile, just a little, feeling excitement quicken her blood.

Here's to new beginnings.

CHAPTER ONE

WHEN THE PILOT announced they were beginning their descent, Chloe leaned closer to the airplane window and was once again disappointed. Thick clouds obscured the view below, just as they had for most of her flights from Heathrow to New York, and from there, toward her final destination: Jamaica.

Jamaica!

Just thinking the name made her smile again. Really, she'd hardly stopped smiling since hearing where she was going as part of the Kensington Project, which sent specialists to other hospitals outside the UK to share their expertise. While she'd expressed interest in the prestigious program months ago, she hadn't been informed of where she was being sent until just recently. And now here she was, on November first, winging her way to her destination.

She'd heard so much about the island but hadn't had a chance to visit, and now her heart raced as she waited to catch her first glimpse of its legendary beauty.

As though sensing her excitement and taking pity, the clouds suddenly thinned, then disappeared, revealing peaks and valleys of an almost startling green.

"Oh!"

Her soft exclamation attracted the attention of the lady next to her, and the older woman looked out the window too.

"It's beautiful, isn't it?" she asked, the pride in her voice evident, her accent definitively Jamaican.

"Lovely," Chloe agreed, giving her a grin before turning back to the window.

"No matter how many times I come back home, every time I see those hills, my heart is happy."

Glad to have someone to share her enthusiasm, Chloe asked, "I'm sure it is, with a view like that to come back to. Were you away for long?"

The lady laughed. "I've lived in New York for the last forty years, but no matter what, I always think of Jamaica as home."

Chloe chuckled. "My gran is the same. She's lived in England for probably sixty years and still talks about Jamaica as though she just left. She was so excited when she heard I was going."

"Is this your first visit?" the lady asked, her

brow creasing as though she couldn't believe it. "Even though your grandmother is Jamaican?"

"It is," Chloe replied, wondering why the other woman thought that was so strange. "Both of my grandparents are Jamaican, but they met in England. Once they started a family, they couldn't afford to go back very often, and although I've wanted to visit, I've not had an opportunity until now."

Besides, Finn hadn't been at all interested in her Jamaican heritage and always vetoed the island as a vacation destination.

"How long will you be visiting?" The lady seemed intent on ferreting out every secret Chloe may possess. "Do you have any family left here, or will you be going to one of the resorts?"

"Actually, I'll be here for two months," Chloe told her, feeling another little tingle of happiness at just saying the words. "And no relatives left, that I know of anyway. It's a working holiday, so I'll be in Jamaica for Christmas. Going by what my gran says, that should be fun."

"Oh, we Jamaicans love Christmas," the lady replied with a decisive nod. "Why do you think I come back almost every year, now that I'm retired? Will you be in town or in the country?"

Not being sure what the lady meant by *town*, Chloe simply answered, "I'll be working at Kingston General Hospital."

"You're a doctor?"

There was no skepticism in her voice. Instead, she was beaming as though that was great news, and her reaction caused a little glow of warmth to bloom in Chloe's chest.

"I am. A neurologist, to be exact."

"How wonderful. Your family must be so proud and pleased."

Then, thankfully, her new acquaintance leaned over and started to point out landmarks below and Chloe didn't have to reply.

The reality was her family members—with the exception of her grandmother—were anything but pleased with her at this point, and that still stung.

When she'd called, excited to share being chosen as a part of the Kensington Project, her mum had been less than enthusiastic.

"We've hardly seen you in months," she'd complained. "First, too busy with work, then off to San Francisco for a conference, and now, hardly back a month and you're off again."

To hear her you'd think Chris Taylor, Chloe's boss, had decided to include Chloe in the project just to spite her mother.

"It's a great opportunity, Mum. I'll get to share some of the research and advancements we've made at the hospital and to see Jamaica at the same time."

"But to be away for Christmas?" Her mum sounded outraged, as though she'd discovered a plot against her and the family. "Why on earth would they send you off into the wilds now?"

"Jamaica is hardly 'the wilds,' Mum—"

"Well, I think it's very poor form, sending folks away over the holidays."

Hearing that particular tone in Mum's voice, Chloe's first impulse was to try to placate her and calm her down. That's what she'd always done, and it was probably expected, but after a lot of thought, she'd decided the habit was one that needed breaking.

Over the years, people—especially her family and Finn—had used her peacemaking tendencies to their own advantages, pushing her into corners with their anger. Hammering at her until, suddenly, she was doing what *they* wanted rather than what was best for her.

So while a litany of complaints flowed from Mum's lips, Chloe hadn't bothered to argue. Instead, she'd let Mum have her head, then reiterated firmly that she'd be going to Jamaica. While that had gone over like a lead balloon, the frosty silence and cool goodbye thereafter had almost been worth it.

Apparently, the expectation was that if you protested hard enough, Chloe would change her plans to accommodate. Well, they'd soon learn she wasn't inclined to give in anymore.

And truthfully, she was glad not to have to deal with that particular battle at Christmas. In the past it had been her favorite time of year. The lights and decorations. Bustling about to find perfect gifts for family and friends.

But since her split with Finn, and the reaction to it from her family, the season had definitely lost its luster. If she spent it with her family again this year, she'd once more be expected to take all comments with grace, as though having her family side with Finn wasn't painful. And if she decided to respond to anyone the way she'd want to, there would be hell to pay.

All things considered, she was glad to avoid fielding the inevitable questions about the divorce, not to mention remarks like those she'd been subjected to at the last family get-together. Aunt Gloria saying it was obvious being single didn't agree with Chloe, since she looked so 'sickly,' while Aunt Janice warned she shouldn't let herself go, since it would be harder to find a new husband.

As though after what Finn had put her through, she had any intention of looking for another relationship, much less getting married!

No.

She was just finding herself again after years of being a part of a couple. Rediscovering facets of her personality she'd forgotten or pushed aside in service of being Finn's wife. Embracing this new life with gusto and the kind of pleasure her family couldn't and wouldn't try to understand.

Like the excitement of a one-night stand with a handsome, sexy man.

Remembering the night in San Francisco gave Chloe a secret, delicious thrill.

It had been, in its own way, revelatory.

She'd only ever been with Finn and would be the first to admit their sex life had grown stale and flat, although she hadn't been able to put her finger on why. Then, when she found out he'd been cheating on her with a work colleague, she'd thought that explained their lackluster lovemaking.

Finn had a different idea about what the problem was.

"You're just not very sexual, Chloe. It's hard to get really excited when the woman you're with doesn't exactly seem to enjoy being made love to."

At least he'd stopped short of calling her "cold," but hearing him say that made her truly angry.

"You never complained before. Why is it, all of a sudden, that *your* cheating is *my* fault?"

As though realizing he was close to saying the unforgivable, he'd tried charm instead.

"Chloe, you know I love you. I always have. But we were so young when we started going out, I got curious about what it would be like with someone else. I made a horrible mistake, but it was a one-off. I'm sure if we work at it, we'll get back to where we were."

That conversation had put the final nail in the coffin of their marriage. Perhaps in time she might have forgiven him for cheating, as she had before. He didn't realize she knew about his previous indiscretions, since she'd kept the knowledge to herself, determined to make their marriage work. After all, she'd put so much into the relationship and had loved Finn for so long, she'd been scared of what it meant for them to no longer be a couple.

But she couldn't forgive him for lying nor for trying to make her the problem when it was clearly him.

Yet his assertion that their issues in bed stemmed from her lack of sexual interest had haunted her and left her with lingering doubts.

But what she'd discovered in San Francisco allayed them, forever.

Just thinking about that wildly passionate night still made her hot and bothered.

First, there was the fact that she'd actually agreed to sleep with a man without knowing anything about him except his first name—if the name he'd given her was even real.

Second, there had been absolutely nothing wrong with her libido when she was in his arms. In fact, she'd been a little shocked at the ferocity of her desires and how demanding she'd become in search of satisfaction.

The day after, as she settled in for the long plane ride back to England, she'd been both relieved to have Finn proven wrong and astounded at her newfound boldness. Yet while she regretted nothing about that night—especially since it had cemented her determination to take more risks—she had no intention of making a habit of picking up strange men. It had been a successful, exhilarating experiment but not one she was sure she felt comfortable repeating.

No, she told herself, as she shook off the memory of that night and tried to bring her wayward breathing back under control. It had been astounding, earth-shattering and brought her to life in a way nothing else could have, but it wasn't a high she'd be chasing often.

Irrespective of the nights spent tossing and turning as her body remembered finding the ultimate satisfaction with a man clearly versed in how to pleasure a woman.

Going forward she had a plan to rebuild her life, which didn't include getting involved, even casually, with any men.

Dragging her thoughts back to the present, she was in time to have her seatmate point out the town of Portmore, which she described as a bedroom community for the capital city, Kingston.

"My daughter lives there," she explained, before pointing out the peninsula where both the airport and Port Royal were located. "You've heard of Port Royal, right? It used to be called the Wickedest City in Christendom before it was mostly destroyed by an earthquake, somewhere back in the seventeenth century. It shrank to a village, but now it's a heritage site with a cruise-ship terminal. They serve some of the best steamed fish there. Make sure you get someone to take you."

And as the pilot announced they were about to land, the lady added, "I hope you have a wonderful time in J.A."

Stuffing the research paper she'd been reading back into her bag, Chloe gave the older woman another wide smile. "Oh, I'm sure I will."

It was just the adventure she needed, and she intended to enjoy every moment.

Dr. Lemuel "Sam" Powell checked his watch, shifting restlessly from foot to foot. Around him swirled the cacophony of the arrivals area at the Norman Manley International Airport. Shouts of welcome, impatient honking of horns and the whistles of the police officers hurrying people along battered his ears, adding to his annoyance.

He was supposed to be at the golf club, playing dominoes and relaxing as he usually did on a Sunday afternoon, not at the airport waiting for a visiting neurologist.

But when the CEO of the hospital had called that Friday and asked for a favor, Sam knew it wasn't in his best interests to say no outright, even if they were also friends. That didn't mean he didn't try his best to get out of the chore.

"Shouldn't Gilbert Owens be meeting him, since he's head of neurology? Or even Dr. James?"

Kendrick Mattison sighed. "Listen, Sam, Owens isn't at all pleased to be hosting a visiting specialist. I think he's taking it as some kind of affront. You know how he can be."

Sam did know. They were extremely lucky to have Dr. Owens on staff and heading up the neurology department. The older man was well respected, both for the research he'd done and his spotless record, but also notoriously hard to please and inclined to take offense if he felt he wasn't being given his due. Perhaps he was wondering why, exactly, the Royal Kensington Hospital felt it would be advantageous to Kingston General to have this Dr. Bailey for two months.

"That's all well and good, but what about Simon James? As your second, he would be a good representative of the hospital."

"He's out of town, and before you even ask, Rashida's mother is throwing her a baby shower, and you know how peed off she'd be if I missed it."

Sam had snorted, trying not to laugh outright. Rashida Mattison was a four-foot-ten dynamo who both terrorized her husband and had him wrapped around her little finger.

"Yeah, laugh all you want, but your day will come," Kendrick said. "And when you're wrapped up in matrimony like I am, I'll be on the sidelines giving laughs for peas soup."

"Well, save your hilarity," Sam replied, letting obvious smugness color his voice. "Because it's not happening."

"Well, happening or happening not, we'll have to see, but I need you at the airport at four to pick up Dr. Bailey. Stop by the office before you leave. One of my admins will have a sign printed for you to hold so she knows who you are."

"She?"

But even as the question left his lips, he realized Kendrick had already hung up.

So with that in mind, Sam had been diligently watching the door, holding up a sign on which was printed Dr. Bailey, trying to spot the English neurologist. But besides one or two curious glances, no one had approached.

Sam shifted again, fighting the restlessness that had plagued him for the last month. This was never his favorite time of year to begin with, since it brought forward memories kept at bay most of the rest of the time by a constant whirl of activity. Company and the camaraderie to be found at the golf club or his favorite bar, where he sometimes went to play darts or pool, helped keep the ghosts asleep.

Being alone in his house made him hyper-aware of the echoing spaces in his head, which, if given the chance, filled with old sorrows and questions he could neither answer nor seem to avoid. This year he'd had a brief respite in the form of an erotic night with a sensual stranger. But while he'd been able to forget Victoria and all that had happened for a few blissful hours, the aftermath had left him even edgier than before.

Lost in thought, Sam jumped as a loud altercation broke out behind him, where cars were stopping to pick up passengers. Spinning around, he saw two drivers arguing, threats and curse words flying left and right. Then a couple of police officers joined the fray while disembarking passengers and other gawkers crowded around to watch the spectacle.

Taking advantage of his height to keep an eye on the melee, Sam held the sign at an angle where it could be seen by people coming out of the doors.

Just as the officers were succeeding in breaking up the quarrel, he heard a strangely familiar voice say, "Sam?"

He froze, as shocked as she sounded, all the air rushing out of his lungs, disbelief holding him in place for a long, fraught moment.

Then he turned and found himself face-to-face

with a woman who'd haunted his nights and be-deviled his days. One he thought he'd never see again after that one ecstatic night.

"Chloe?"

Her mouth had been open just a bit, obviously in disbelief, but at his question, it firmed. Grew almost grim.

"Yes. Dr. Chloe Bailey. I believe you're here to pick me up?"

CHAPTER TWO

CHLOE HAD STOPPED so abruptly, the porter had to swerve to avoid running into her heels with his trolley. Trying desperately to maintain some kind of composure, she locked her trembling knees and wiped as much expression from her face as she was able to, though her skin felt clammy and cold.

Even as she'd said his name, she'd been sure she was wrong—had expected him to turn and tell her she was mistaken. Surely when she saw him full face, she'd see her error and he'd look nothing at all like the man she'd slept with in San Francisco.

But instead, she was gobsmacked to realize it definitely was him, in the flesh, staring back at her with a look of intense shock. If she weren't so flabbergasted herself, she'd be inclined to laugh at his expression, but amusement was the last thing on her mind.

Even as her brain whirled with questions she was too stunned to ask, she was taking in every remembered feature of Sam's face.

The soft dark skin, his chin shaded with a hint of stubble, as it had been the night they'd spent together.

Wide-set eyes, with their almost black irises and ridiculously thick lashes.

The intelligent sweep of his forehead, eyebrows tipped high up in surprise.

Strong nose and jawline.

And that perfect, full-lipped mouth…

Focusing on those lips caused heat to explode in her belly and fan out over every inch of her body. All too well did she remember the deliciously wicked things his mouth—incongruously both soft and firm at the same time—was capable of. Fighting for control, Chloe tore her gaze away, reluctantly meeting his once more.

Yet Sam seemed as tongue-tied as she herself was, and who knew how long they might have stood there staring at each other if the porter hadn't intervened.

"Boss, we have-fi move. We blocking the way."

Sam blinked a couple times as though waking up, then looked at the porter.

"Yes," he said, his voice strained, like his throat was tight. "Take the lady to a spot on the curb, please, while I go for my car."

Then without another word, he turned on his heel and walked away, leaving Chloe to stare as he disappeared into the crowd.

"This way, miss," the porter said, swinging

his trolley around her with an expert twist of his body.

Still reeling from the unexpected encounter, Chloe blindly followed the porter to a clear area on the pavement, where he started unloading her bags.

Despite the heat of the afternoon, she was shivering, her brain scrambling to come to terms with what she'd seen.

San Francisco Sam? Here?

No doubt working at the same hospital she was assigned to for the next two months?

How?

Why?

"You all right, miss?" The porter's question shook her out of her muddled thoughts, and she turned to see him watching her, concern clearly etched in his face. "You need to sit down?"

His solicitude brought her back to herself, and she took a deep, steadying breath.

"No, I'll be okay. Thank you." Finally remembering she had to pay him, she unzipped her handbag and rooted about for her purse. She retrieved a banknote and held it out.

"I'll stay here with you until your man comes back," he said, as he took the money from her hand.

Knowing the elderly porter was only being nice, Chloe bit her tongue so as not to snap that Sam was *not* her man.

Instead, she managed to dredge up a smile from somewhere and replied, "That's very kind of you but not necessary. I'll be fine."

But the porter only leaned on his trolley and tipped back his red cap.

"No problem, miss." The corners of his eyes crinkled as he smiled back. "Yuh remind mi of mi granddaughter. Mi nuh mind staying for a little, till you feel better."

And his gentle waffling about the weather and then his family had the benefit of calming her down. Her laughter at one of his stories about his son loosened her muscles, releasing the tension locking them.

Yet as soon as the vehicle pulled up in front of her and Sam got out of the driver's side, all the stress came flooding back.

She stood silently as the two men casually chatted while stowing her suitcases in the back of his 4X4. Sam even chuckled, as though nothing untoward had taken place, seemingly completely unconcerned about seeing her again.

Then he glanced her way and caught her staring. A flash, like lightning, jolted down her spine. Miffed at herself and his insouciance, she called out her thanks to the porter and opened the door to enter the vehicle. Once in the passenger seat, she pulled out her dark glasses and put them on, blocking both the tropical glare and Sam's gaze.

Hopefully they'd hide whatever he might be able to read in her eyes.

What to do now? Bring up their prior meeting or wait for Sam to do so? There were so many questions she wanted to ask, but her emotions were all over the place and she was too flustered to figure out how best to approach the issue.

Never in a million years had she expected to see this man again, and ridiculously, her brain ping-ponged between pleasure and an emotion too close to fear to be comfortable.

When Sam got into the driver's seat, Chloe kept her gaze trained ahead, looking out the windscreen at the swirling crowd of people and vehicles. Yet it was impossible not to see his movements in her peripheral vision, and although she briefly thought about turning to look out the passenger-side window instead, she didn't.

In fact, as he buckled his seatbelt, she realized she was looking at him from the corner of her eye. When he put the vehicle in gear, the breath hitched in her throat at the sight of his strong, long-fingered hand, her body remembering with startling clarity the sensations it had created.

And the memory was delicious.

Dragging her eyes away, she stared straight ahead again as Sam maneuvered the car through the throng and away from the departure area.

The silence lay thick between them, and Chloe was reluctant to break it. What would be worse, driving into Kingston in silence or engaging in discussion about this unbelievable encounter?

He'd left the airport behind and they'd traversed a roundabout before he said even a word.

"Well, this is a surprise."

From his tone it obviously wasn't a pleasant one, and a wave of heat—part embarrassment, part annoyance—flooded up into Chloe's face.

"For me, too," she said, keeping her voice level as best she could, hoping he didn't hear it wobble at the end.

"Really?"

Now he sounded downright skeptical, and as Chloe turned to look at him, she had to rein in rising anger, although some leaked through when she asked, "What are you implying?" Despite her best efforts, her voice rose. "That I followed you here?"

He was silent for a long moment, but his mouth tightened, lines forming at the corners as he frowned.

Finally, he said, "Well, what are the odds of us meeting a month ago in San Francisco and then you suddenly turning up in Jamaica?"

Astounded at his arrogance, all Chloe could do was stare. Then anger turned to ice-cold rage, all embarrassment disappearing.

"Get your ego under control," she snapped. "You're making yourself look like a git."

"I'm…" he sputtered, his head whipping about

with satisfying alacrity to give her a shocked glance. "What—?"

"First off," she butted in, unrepentant at interrupting whatever he wanted to say, glad he'd looked back at the road ahead, releasing her from his dark gaze. "I didn't get to choose where Royal Kensington was sending me and didn't know I was coming here until a few days ago. Secondly, I didn't even know you were Jamaican when we met last month. You sounded American—"

"I don't sound American at all."

"You certainly did when we were talking at the bar," she retorted, wondering if he'd put on the accent then, although she still heard a trace of it now. "And, since we didn't get around to exchanging life stories, I assumed you were American."

"All that is well and good, but—"

On a roll, she spoke right over him, so incensed the words tumbled over one another.

"Finally, and most importantly—if I *were* interested in anything more than what we shared that night, wouldn't I have at least given you my contact information before leaving?"

Sam's mouth opened and closed a couple of times, but all that came out was an inarticulate sound. Satisfied she'd made her point, Chloe crossed her arms and firmly turned her head away, glad her words had at least seemed to shut him up.

* * *

Sam gripped the steering wheel so hard his knuckles hurt. He definitely wasn't used to being raked over the coals—except by his mother on occasion—and his first impulse was a swift, harsh rebuttal.

Why was she so surprised that he'd think she'd followed him to Jamaica? Wasn't it the kind of coincidence no one would believe? He was well within his rights to question her motivations.

Except, deep down he knew he actually deserved the tongue lashing he'd just received.

He'd been shocked when he turned around and saw her, and he knew without a doubt he wasn't the only one rocked by the encounter. Her eyes had been wide with surprise and her lips parted as though she were trying to speak but couldn't. But more than just being stunned by the sight of her here in Jamaica, Sam was even more dumbfounded by his instinctive reaction.

He'd wanted to grab, hug and kiss her. Take that luscious mouth beneath his, claiming it the way he had back in San Francisco.

One-night stands weren't something he usually indulged in, simply because they were inherently risky. Although, having long ago decided he wouldn't get seriously involved with anyone again, he made sure to steer clear of anything that seemed as if it might become a relationship.

Instead, there'd been short-term flings or brief affairs.

What was strange about the San Francisco encounter was how hard it had been to get Chloe out of his mind. For a month he'd been trying to forget about her, but her memory had refused to be banished. That night had been an amazing, erotic experience, and the sheer sensuality of it invaded his thoughts with arousing and annoying regularity.

Now having been taken to task, he had to admit his response to her arrival back into his life had been brought on by an emotion he had no name for but somehow resented nonetheless.

His ruminations were interrupted by the need to hit the brakes as a fast-moving vehicle overtook his, squeezing into the lane ahead to avoid hitting an oncoming minibus. Realizing he wasn't giving the road the concentration it needed, he put on his indicator and pulled over to the curb, just past Gunboat Beach.

As he put the vehicle into park, Sam suppressed a sigh, dreading the upcoming confrontation.

Oh, he knew she was probably telling the truth. Everything she'd said had sounded convincing, and indignation had rung in her outraged tone. However, whether she was being completely honest, he had no way to know. He was in the habit of viewing coincidences and other people's words with a jaundiced eye.

Especially when the person involved was a woman.

That was a lesson he'd learned a long time ago and didn't need reminding of.

Chloe was still looking out the passenger window, her gaze seemingly fixed on Kingston Harbor or perhaps on the city beyond. With her arms tightly crossed over her chest, and the rather haughty tilt of her nose, her annoyance couldn't be clearer.

Well, he was annoyed too. Sam tried to convince himself it was because Chloe might suddenly expect there to be something more between them rather than anything else.

What on earth else could be causing this swirling emotion, which made it so hard to be conciliatory?

The sudden memory of her saying if she'd wanted anything more than that one night she'd have made her wishes clear had to be pushed aside. Sam took a steadying breath in preparation for wading into what felt like turbulent waters, but before he could even marshal his thoughts, Chloe rounded on him again. The expression of horror on her face made his heart rate pick up.

"Hello! Tell me you're not in neurology."

"I'm not," he replied, hearing the stiffness in his own tone. "I'm a surgeon."

"Oh, thank goodness."

She turned away again, leaving him once more speechless and even more embarrassed. Even though he didn't want her to think they could pick back up where they had left off, he also didn't want any awkwardness between them to seep through into the hospital. But where to start? Then he remembered one of her points and decided that was as good a place as any.

"Listen, I might have sounded American because I went to school there, from when I was seventeen until I finished my residency. It's not inconceivable that I fall back into the old speech patterns when I go back."

She threw him a narrow-eyed look, her lips pursed, but didn't reply, just turned to stare out the window again.

Then, before he could figure how best to continue, Chloe asked, "I take it that's Kingston over there?"

Apparently, she had no interest in continuing their prior conversation, and Sam couldn't decide whether to be annoyed or relieved.

"Yes, it is," he replied, leaning forward to point past her toward Victoria Pier, on the other side of the harbor. Dusk was falling and lights were beginning to come on, showing the sweep of the city climbing the hills in the distance. "That's downtown Kingston there and the corporate area spreading out behind. If you look past Long Mountain, over there, you can just make out the start of the Blue Mountains."

She seemed intent on examining the view, and Sam once again considered if he should say anything more. He should be pleased she seemed disinclined to discuss the strange circumstance they found themselves in, but something niggled at him. Whether it was conscience or a totally different impulse, he didn't know. All he knew was the entire situation had thrown him for a loop, and until he'd had a chance to sort through the events of the afternoon, he'd rather not say the wrong thing.

Again.

Yet he knew his attitude hadn't set the best stage for any future meetings and he should swallow his pride and apologize.

"Listen, let's just start over." In San Francisco she'd said she liked his smile, so when she finally turned to face him, he gave her one of his best.

She frowned in return.

Not particularly encouraging, but he forged ahead nonetheless.

"I'm not trying to make excuses, but seeing you like this has really thrown me."

He wished he could see her eyes, because perhaps then he'd have a better idea what she was thinking. Instead, all he saw was his own face reflected back at him in her shades, and the image of what looked like a leer on his face had his grin fading to nothing.

"Right," she said, and there was no mistaking the sharp tone. "It'll suit me to pretend we'd never met before."

Then she turned away again, leaving him with the impression the conversation was satisfactorily over.

Taking in a deep breath through his nose, Sam checked his mirrors and merged back into the fast-moving traffic.

"Oh." He suddenly remembered he'd been tasked with another job. Seeing her had driven it from his mind. "I was given a package for you. It's on the back seat, so please don't let me forget it when I drop you off."

She twisted to look into the rear of the vehicle.

"I see it," she said, before leaning between the front seats. "I think I can reach it."

She brushed his shoulder, leaving a hot, tingling spot behind. The scent of her hair rushed into his nostrils, bringing memories of burying his face in it as he shuddered with pleasure, trying not to lose control.

As she settled back into her seat, Sam realized it wasn't just the heavy Kingston traffic that was going to make the drive to Chloe's apartment a long one.

His heightened awareness, and the attendant desire raging through his blood, was going to make it everlasting.

CHAPTER THREE

CHLOE MANAGED TO hold it all together until Sam finally dropped her off at the flat the hospital had arranged for her. Then she collapsed onto the nearest chair and rubbed her nape.

The entire encounter had left her shaken, annoyed and—she was forced to admit—aroused.

When she thought there was no chance of ever seeing Sam again, she'd allowed herself to cast him in the role of perfect fantasy man. The kind of memory and image she'd be able to call on during those times when she was moved to pleasure herself in lieu of risking another anonymous encounter.

Now, having come face-to-face with him, she knew if they met again, it would take monumental willpower to continue the casually distant act she'd assumed for the rest of the drive.

Thankfully, she'd had the package from Kingston General to concentrate on, and it had, in turn, led to several topics of conversation she could effortlessly broach.

In the big manila envelope she'd found keys, a cell phone and a very nice letter from Kendrick Mattison, the hospital CEO, apologizing for not meeting her at the airport himself. At first, she'd been annoyed that he hadn't made the effort, thereby sparing her this uncomfortable journey. Then it came home to her how much more embarrassing it might have been had she and Sam seen each other for the first time at the hospital. Likely they'd have been surrounded by people who would surely have noticed their stunned reactions.

No, she decided. As shocking as this first meeting had been, far better for it to have been in private, than the alternative of having an audience.

The cell phone had been procured and activated by the hospital for her use while on the island and had been programmed with some numbers they thought she should have.

There would be a dinner to welcome her the following evening, and she would officially start at the hospital on Tuesday, giving her time to recover from her journey. Also, there were additional plans for her stay, covered separately in the attached itinerary.

Turning to the itinerary, she scanned the list. Along with the promised dinner, there was an orientation tour of the hospital on Tuesday morning. Reading further, she got a bit of a shock.

"Oh, they've arranged for me to do an interview with a newspaper. I wasn't expecting that."

Sam shrugged. "I'm not surprised. Having you here is a coup for Kingston General."

"Really?" She hadn't considered that an aspect of her trip. To her, it was simply a way to disseminate knowledge. "Why?"

He'd sent her a sideways glance, as though trying to figure out whether she was being disingenuous. Obviously whatever he saw in her expression had him taking her question seriously.

"Kingston General is a fairly new hospital, founded five years ago on the site of an older hospital that closed. Although it's classified as a private hospital, the aim has always been to offer specialized services to those who otherwise couldn't afford them, through a referral system. As a result, attracting specialists who can diagnose and treat less-prevalent diseases has always been a priority. Having a neurologist visiting from the UK, who's here to share new techniques and treatment options, is definitely something to advertise."

"I suppose so," she'd replied slowly, tamping down a nervous chill. "But I'm not used to being interviewed. Hopefully I do Royal Kensington and Kingston General—and myself—credit."

Sam sent her a smile. "I'm sure you'll be fine," he'd replied.

Blindly looking back down at the papers in

her hand, she'd cursed herself as desire cascaded through her system, banishing her nerves and pretty much shorting out her brain.

He really had the most amazing smile.

It took her a moment to gather her thoughts.

"So health care isn't free here?"

"It is, in the public hospitals, but wait times can be long, and there's always been a demand for alternatives. Private hospitals fill that need."

"So there's a disparity in care?"

"There can be," he said slowly. "Wealthy patients can choose where they go and use a private doctor or surgeon, while everyone else has to wait. Which is why Kingston General is set up the way it is. Today I operated on a young boy with a bowel obstruction, from an inner-city community. He'd been referred from the public hospital because they didn't have a surgeon on hand and the case was urgent.

"It's always been the mandate that we don't turn patients away because of an inability to pay, but we usually only take referrals."

"What about medication costs?"

Shop talk seemed a safe enough subject, particularly since he was driving and had to keep a sharp eye on the roads. Originally, Chloe had considered renting a car, but if the Kingston traffic was anything to go by, she wasn't sure she'd feel confident about driving here. Drivers seemed inclined to do whatever they wanted, whenever it occurred to them, without use of indicators or, it seemed, their brake pedals. Luckily, the letter from Dr. Mattison included the information that the hospital had arranged for her to have a driver taking her back and forth to work during the week.

"Many medications are dispensed free of cost through the public hospitals and clinics, and there are a number of health-insurance schemes patients pay into to mitigate costs at pharmacies."

She'd continued to pepper him with work questions for the rest of the journey, not wanting silence to fall between them or, worse, to have him revert to their previous conversation. They'd actually passed the hospital, which he'd pointed out to her, and when he turned into the driveway of the small apartment complex, she realized it was only about ten minutes away from Kingston General.

"I could walk to work," she said, as she unbuckled her seatbelt. "It's close enough."

Sam paused with one foot out of the vehicle and gave her a stern look. "I wouldn't advise it."

"Why not?" Normally she'd be willing to take advice, but for some reason, she was reluctant to give Sam any leeway. Silly as it may seem, his very existence made her want to be contrary.

"It might not be safe."

"Why not?" she asked again, a little more forcefully. "It's probably, what, about three miles?

And it seemed I'd be walking through a mostly residential area and then on a main road. I don't see the problem."

He was frowning, and although it should have been unattractive, Chloe's heart started pounding at the way his face fell into severe lines. He was suddenly even more gorgeous, and she couldn't help resenting him for it.

"Like most other cities in the world, Kingston can be dangerous to those who don't know it well. This isn't a tourist area, or out in the country where people look out for others. I'm sure the hospital made arrangements regarding your transportation, and it would be best if you took advantage of that."

She hadn't answered, just ignored the heat running along her spine and frowned back at him before getting out of the car.

He'd pulled her bags from the back of the vehicle, and they made their way into the building, using the keys Dr. Mattison had sent for her. The flat she was in was on the third floor, and her awareness of Sam was almost intolerable in the close proximity of the small elevator.

Trying to pull her thoughts away from reaching out, touching him to see if his skin was as soft as she remembered, was a battle that left her silent, tongue-tied with an intense surge of arousal.

Wrapped in his scent, seeing his reflection in

the stainless-steel walls, made it far too easy for the memories to flood in.

Tell me what you want.

His voice had been hoarse. His hand, which moments before had been sliding across her breast, had stilled, making her back arch with the desire to have the sinfully tormenting caresses continue.

Touch me, she'd demanded, before telling him exactly where, and how hard, and for how long.

Alone now, no longer needing to keep up her facade of unconcern, Chloe dropped her head into her hands, not sure whether to laugh or cry. The woman who'd had sex with Sam in San Francisco had been hardly recognizable. There had been no way to reconcile her with the old Chloe, who'd been passive and content to take whatever Finn gave rather than insisting on satisfaction.

While she'd been determined to hold on to the boost of confidence and personal power the night had brought out in her, she'd given no thought to what might happen should they meet again.

What she wanted was to call her best friend, Cora, and spill the entire story—including the encounter in San Francisco. Chloe had hugged the memory of that night close, wanting to savor it for a while before talking about it with anyone. Before she'd got to the stage where she was willing to share, both she and Cora had been chosen for the Kensington Project. Right now, Cora was in Stockholm, Sweden, where it would already be—Chloe checked her watch—after midnight. There was no way she would wake Cora up for this.

Besides, she told herself sternly as she got up to start moving her bags to the bedroom, she wasn't a child. She could handle it and whatever else came her way without anyone's support.

And, as she'd calmly told Sam before he left, since they wouldn't be directly working together, they probably wouldn't meet again.

At least, she heartily hoped so, for her own peace of mind.

Sam started the vehicle and sat for a moment, trying to sort out his thoughts—which Dr. Chloe Bailey had sent into a tailspin. He was positively flummoxed from seeing her again, his body taut, his heart still pounding although he was no longer in close proximity to the temptation she presented.

The last time he'd felt this confused and discombobulated, he'd been battling with grief and disbelief...

He tried pushing the thought away, shocked that it had even come to mind, although he shouldn't be.

Although the two instances had nothing in common, beyond this strange fight-or-flight impulse, he'd just been thinking about Victoria at the airport.

The car crash had been eight years ago, but every year around the time of that dreadful anniversary, the memories grew stronger—the agony harder to bear.

Yet ironically, without the lingering pain of Victoria's death—and that of the child he hadn't even known she was carrying—he probably wouldn't have slept with Chloe that night in California.

The sorrow still haunted him. Worse yet was not knowing why she'd withheld from him the fact she was pregnant. Every year he asked himself the interminable and unanswerable questions. Where had Victoria been going? Why—at four months pregnant—hadn't she told him about the baby? What else hadn't he been aware of in their relationship?

Was it something about him that had made her keep something so important and life changing to herself?

Had he inadvertently caused the disaster?

There was no way to know. Vicky had taken her secrets with her when she died. None of her friends had seemed to know what was going on and had declared themselves as shocked as he was. He'd met her brother a couple of times, but the siblings hadn't been particularly close, and when they saw each other at her funeral, the other man said he hadn't talked to his sister in months.

All of those memories had been bombarding him in San Francisco, and he'd been once more battling with them the night he'd seen Chloe across the bar. It was what had drawn him to her and led to that night of exquisite pleasure.

Pleasure that had driven the demons back into hiding and rendered Sam, in a strange and unfathomable way, renewed.

The old pain had been dulled, replaced by a memory of a woman so responsive, so intensely passionate he'd begun to wonder if he'd ever be able to forget her.

And now here she was. Slated to work in the same hospital he was in for two long months.

But Chloe had been right when she said they probably wouldn't see much of each other during her stay. They worked in different specialties and even would be in different wings of the hospital, so there was no need to come into contact, and they really could pretend they'd never met before.

Instead of making him feel better, the thought annoyed him more than anything else.

Dammit, the best thing he could do—for his sanity and his temper—was to forget he'd ever met Dr. Chloe Bailey and get on with his life.

Pulling out his phone, he sent Kendrick Mattison a text to let him know the visiting neurologist was safely at her apartment. Normally he'd call, but he had no interest in talking to his good friend right now. Not with all these crazy thoughts and feelings crashing about inside. Kendrick would hear in his voice that there was something off and demand to know what it was.

With a grim chuckle, he put the car in gear. Pulling out onto the road, he headed north out of the area adjacent to New Kingston toward his home above Manor Park. He'd just turned up the volume on his radio when the phone rang. Not wanting to answer but knowing it didn't make sense to avoid it, he hit the hands-free button to connect the call.

"Hey Kendrick. What's up?"

"I wanted to make sure everything went okay this afternoon."

He sounded rushed, and there was talk and laughter in the background, making it difficult to hear him.

"Yep. She arrived as scheduled, and I just dropped her off at the apartment as ordered."

Making sure he kept his voice even and casual took effort. He'd just decided to forget all about the darned woman, and here was an immediate—and completely unwanted—reminder of her existence.

"What's she like?"

Beautiful. Sexy. Infuriating.

"I didn't spend *that* much time with her," he temporized.

Kendrick made an impatient sound. "Just your general impression."

Sam bit back a sigh. "Seems nice enough."

"What?" Kendrick was practically roaring over the noise behind him, and Sam heard him kiss his teeth. "Listen, I'll talk to you later, or tomorrow. I can hardly hear you. I don't know why we have to go through this again."

Sam chuckled at his friend's disgruntled tone, knowing that for all his grousing, Kendrick didn't mind. He was a devoted husband and father. They may be expecting their third child, but Sam knew Kendrick was just as excited as he had been about the first.

That thought brought a pang of melancholy, which had to be ruthlessly suppressed as they said their goodbyes.

Sam drummed his fingers on the wheel, trying to decide whether to go straight home or not. The dominoes crew would still be at the clubhouse, and while the tournament would be well underway, they'd be company.

But at the same time, Sam wasn't sure he actually wanted company, or for someone to notice how out of sorts he was. Being alone at home would definitely be better than having to answer any nosy questions regarding his mood.

It was a clear choice between his own company and thoughts and whatever distraction his friends could provide. But since, despite being

Sunday, traffic was crawling along Waterloo Road, it wasn't a decision that needed to be made right away.

His phone rang again, but this time he didn't mind the distraction.

"Mel, how're you?"

His sister let out an exaggerated sigh. "Frazzled. Allison had a meltdown of titanic proportions this evening when we wouldn't let her go to the movies with friends. Peter wanted to give in, but I put my foot down. She can't just throw a fit whenever she doesn't get her way, hoping her father will be afraid it'll bring on a seizure and let her do whatever she wants."

Sam could clearly hear the worry beneath his sister's exasperation, and his own stress level rose. His niece's epilepsy was a constant source of concern for the entire family, and Sam was often asked to explain things, both to the adults and to his niece, as well.

"Do you want me to speak to Ali about her behavior, from a medical perspective?" he asked.

Melanie hesitated for a moment and then said, "No. Let me talk to her first. If that doesn't work, maybe I'll ask you to try."

Sam was honest enough to recognize the wash of relief for what it was. Not that he didn't want to speak to Ali about her behavior, but he'd rather see if it became a health threat before he did. She was eleven, on the verge of puberty, and his speaking to her may exacerbate the issue, making teenage rebellion kick in, causing her to ignore his counsel.

One never knew how situations like that might play out.

"What I really called you about is Mummy's charity ball. Did you arrange for the bartenders and drinks?"

"Yes," he replied, glad of the change of subject. "And before you ask, David says he'll send the orchids up from the farm the evening before the party. Send me the florist's address so his delivery driver knows where to go."

"Great, thanks. I'll text it to you." In the background, he heard his brother-in-law's voice, and then Mel said, "I've got to go. See you on the weekend?"

"Sure. I promised to do Sunday dinner with Mummy and Daddy. Will you all be there?"

"Of course," she replied. "Okay, love you. Bye."

By the time he ended the call, he was driving up Constant Spring Road. Here the traffic was a lighter, and now he needed to decide about his destination.

In his mind's eye he pictured his living room, empty and silent. Then, before he knew what was happening, that image was replaced by one of Chloe Bailey. Not as he'd last seen her as the apartment door closed but as he'd seen her in San Francisco.

Naked.

Aroused.

Beckoning him closer. Making him wild with need.

Cursing under his breath, he put on his indicator and turned into the golf-club driveway.

Decision made.

CHAPTER FOUR

UNFORTUNATELY, CHLOE'S PLAN to not see Sam Powell again while in Jamaica was shattered the very next evening when he pulled up outside the building to take her to her welcome dinner.

"What the dickens?" she muttered to herself before walking out of the building, trying to ignore the way her body heated as he got out of his vehicle. Kendrick Mattison hadn't mentioned who was collecting her this evening, but Sam would have been her last thought.

He'd nodded emphatically the evening before when she'd said they probably wouldn't meet again, and she'd taken heart from his agreement.

Yet here he was, turning up again like a bad penny.

Silly to be glad that because she wasn't sure of the dress code she'd erred on the side of semi-formal and thought she looked particularly nice, if she might say so herself.

"Before you say anything," Sam said, as he

came around to open her door. "This wasn't my idea. Kendrick asked me to pick you up."

"It doesn't matter," she lied, keeping her voice cool and even.

"Well, I know you have no interest in being in my company," he replied. "But Kendrick wanted to be at the hotel early and asked me to swing by for you. If I'd refused, he'd definitely have asked me why, and I didn't think you'd want me to go into it with him."

It was on the tip of her tongue to agree, but once more the urge to be contrary came over her.

As she got into the passenger seat, she said, "I don't see why we couldn't say we met at the conference in San Francisco. We don't have to go into details, but it might be easier to let people know we're not complete strangers."

He paused, giving her a searching glance, but she turned away to buckle her seatbelt, unwilling to hold his dark gaze a moment longer than necessary. Bad enough to have been up half the night, the memories of the time they'd spent together making sleep elusive until jetlag and exhaustion had overwhelmed her senses. She still felt unsteady, on high alert, and looking into his eyes, shaded by those luxurious lashes, only heightened her disquiet.

But as he closed her door and started around the car, she took a deep breath and willed her heart rate to slow.

To survive being around Sam without making an ass of herself, she needed to be cool and collected. She'd rather eat bugs than let him know how off-kilter she was in his proximity.

As he got into the driver's seat, Chloe opened her clutch and checked to make sure she'd remembered to put her small pill case, stocked with anti-inflammatory pain medication, into the bag. When Sam pulled his door shut, she had to resist the childish impulse to hold her breath so the delicious scent of his cologne wouldn't penetrate her senses, but it was already too late.

Her body reacted as though touched, heating and tightening.

Get a hold of yourself, girl!

"You may be right," he said, as he put the vehicle into gear, pulling her out of her thoughts and back to the conversation. "Although Kendrick Mattison will ask why I didn't mention it before. I've spoken to him since I picked you up at the airport."

Chloe waved a hand in his general direction without looking his way. "Just tell him you met so many doctors at the conference, you didn't immediately remember me."

He snorted, the sound a mixture of amusement and what appeared to be derision. "Yeah, I'm sure he'll believe that."

Risking a glance at him, she sent him a frown

but was secretly relieved when he was concentrating on the road.

"What do you mean?"

"I mean, you're a gorgeous woman. No man is going to believe I met you and then forgot. That's not how it works."

Chloe shook her head, ridiculously pleased to be so characterized but also ready to argue. Then, wondering what it was about him that made her so cranky, she thought better of it. "Well, tell him whatever you want. I don't care. But if it comes up, I *will* mention that we met before. I don't see the benefit in pretending otherwise."

"Okay. Okay." There was no mistaking the sharpness of his tone. "If it comes up, I'll say the same, but I won't volunteer the information."

"Fine." She was rather pleased with how unconcerned she sounded. Not at all as though her heart was galloping along.

And she was equally happy when, not long after that, he turned into a driveway just five minutes away from where they'd started.

"What is this place?" she asked, admiring the verdant gardens, artfully groomed and accented by low lights shining up into the trees and casting the various shrubs into fantastical, shadowy shapes.

"It's a hotel," Sam said, steering the car under a portico. "With a fine dining restaurant and a small nightclub. They also have a few private rooms available for functions. It used to be someone's home, I think, back in the days of gracious old mansions in the colonial style."

When the car stopped, a valet stepped forward to open her door, giving her a wide smile and saying, "Good evening, miss."

"Good evening. And thank you."

"I'm going to park, then I'll be back to walk you in," Sam said, as she got out. "Won't be a minute."

Walking into the lobby, Chloe took a moment to catch her breath. Stepping over to a large colorful painting, she pretended to study it while willing herself to calm.

This was a work function, and she'd have to be on her toes. It would be naïve to think everyone would be pleased at the thought of her being here. The CEO of Royal Kensington had even said as much.

"There may be some staff members who view your arrival as an intrusion," he'd warned. "Or that you've been sent because we think their facilities and methods are somehow backward. It'll be up to you to prove that you haven't been sent to 'save' the neurology department or that you consider the way they operate to be outdated. You're simply there to share information that may be helpful to them, based on the research we've been doing."

This first meeting with the doctors would be

key in setting the tone, and she couldn't allow anything to put her off her game.

Especially not the incredible distraction Sam Powell presented.

Hearing the doors behind her open, she glanced toward them and silently cursed as her heart stuttered.

Why did Sam—dressed in a perfectly fitted suit, his loose, sexy stride somehow emphasizing his masculinity—have to be so damned attractive?

Worse when she considered what was beneath that suit…

"Do you like that painting?"

He was standing right behind her, and she had to stop herself from shivering at his low-voiced question.

"It's brilliant," she said sincerely. "I'd love to see more of the artist's work."

He didn't immediately reply, and the brief silence seemed to hum with electricity.

"There are other paintings by him in the National Gallery downtown. If you get a chance to go there, I think you'd enjoy it."

Why did his voice have to be so smooth—rich and dark like the finest chocolate? It made her want to drink it in, let it seduce her into all kinds of wickedly naughty adventures.

Chloe tightened her grip on her bag and fiercely reminded herself this was not a date…

Erotic images immediately arose in her head, causing her breath to hitch.

She knew only too well where a date with Sam could lead, but that would never happen again.

Tilting her chin up, she turned, intent on telling him they should get going, but the dark fire gleaming in his eyes caused the words to dry up in her mouth.

Then, in a blink, what seemed to be carnal interest on his part disappeared, leaving her to wonder if it had actually even existed, and Sam stepped back before offering her his arm.

"We should go in."

His voice was as unruffled as a slow-moving stream, and Chloe forced aside her hesitation to take the proffered elbow.

"Of course. Let's."

As they stepped through the door into the banquet room, Sam realized he was proud to have Chloe on his arm and tried—without much success—to curb the feeling.

They weren't together because they wanted to be but because of happenstance, and he knew he'd best be remembering that.

However, knowing that didn't negate the fact she was fabulous and, with that slightly pugnacious tilt of her chin, carried herself like a queen.

In her high heels she was almost as tall as he was, and the silky dress she was wearing hugged every luscious inch of her curvy figure while baring the smooth skin of her shoulders. Not just elegant, her outfit was meant to draw attention. From the brightly patterned material to the glittery gems on her sandals, her ensemble screamed confidence.

And confidence was extremely sexy in Sam's book.

As soon as they walked into the room, Kendrick came toward them, Rashida following on his heels.

"Ah, Dr. Bailey. I'm Kendrick Mattison. So nice to finally meet you."

As she shook Kendrick's hand, Rashida came up and introductions were made.

"I adore how tall you are," Rashida exclaimed, in her usual no-holds-barred way. "So stately and gorgeous. I've always wanted to be tall."

Chloe laughed, shaking her head. "You probably wouldn't feel that way if you had to go through the geeky, tripping-over-your-own-feet stage I did as a teenager."

"Well, you grew into your height perfectly. And I love that you don't hesitate to wear heels too."

Chloe stuck out one foot, showing her trim ankle and prettily painted toenails. Sam found himself staring and couldn't help wondering if he'd suddenly developed a foot fetish, since he found the sight so enticing.

"Oh, my ex-husband was only an inch or two taller than me and he complained if I wore shoes that made me taller than him. One of the first things I did after we split up was buy myself a whole new shoe wardrobe, all with high heels."

"You're my kind of woman," Rashida said, wrapping her arm through Chloe's and leading her away. "Let me introduce you around."

Sam was treated to the lovely sight of Chloe from the rear, hips swinging, her laughter floating back to him. The entire package was as intoxicating as twelve-year-old rum.

Kendrick's snort of annoyance brought Sam out of the spell he'd fallen under, and Sam tore his gaze away to look at his friend.

"Trust Rashida to just waltz off with Dr. Bailey, taking over my job." He sent Sam a piercing look. "And you didn't tell me she was a looker. I'd have thought that would be your first comment."

Seeing what could be made into an opening to come clean, Sam said, "We'd actually met before, and it didn't occur to me you'd want to hear what she looked like."

Now Kendrick's gaze sharpened until it could cut. "When did you meet her?"

It was clear he was looking for an in-depth explanation, but Sam didn't bite.

"She was at the conference in San Francisco. We met briefly."

"How briefly?"

Looking for a way out of the conversation, Sam said, "Shouldn't you introduce Chloe to Gilbert? You know how he can take offense if he feels slighted in any way."

Kendrick's gaze swung from Sam's carefully questioning face to where Chloe and Rashida were standing, talking to a small group of people, and then back again.

"We'll get back to our conversation later," he threatened, before striding away to scoop Chloe up and lead her toward where Gilbert Owens and his wife were standing.

Sam followed. He'd wondered if he should warn Chloe about the older neurologist's attitude toward having her at the hospital, but then he'd decided to let her handle it her own way. That didn't mean he wasn't interested in seeing how she managed.

He got to the group in time to hear Chloe say, "Dr. Owens, it's such an honor to be able to work with you. When I heard I was coming to Jamaica and realized you were in charge of the neurology department at Kingston General, I was so pleased."

Gilbert Owens looked unmoved as he replied, "That's kind of you."

"Not at all," Chloe said, her smile wide and her eyes sparkling. She was clearly ignoring the frost in his tone. "I read your paper on early-onset dementia a few years after you published it, and that was then I decided to become not just a doctor but a neurologist."

Gilbert's skepticism was palpable. "That paper was published in the 1990s. You couldn't have been out of your teens yet."

"I wasn't," Chloe admitted. "But my grandfather had just been diagnosed with it, and I realized my grandmother was having a very hard time understanding what was happening. I started reading up on the disease, and on a trip to a university medical library, I found your paper." She gave a smile—soft and almost shy—and continued, "I didn't understand much of it at the time, but with a *lot* of effort, I eventually was able to help Gran and Granddad by suggesting ways to keep him engaged, using your research as a template."

It was like watching someone fall in love, Sam thought, as all the starch went out of Gilbert's face, and his lips twitched.

"Well, I've had a chance to do some investigation, too, and I'm glad to know neurological research plays such a big part in the work you're doing at Royal Kensington. I'm particularly interested in what you've discovered about limbic-predominant, age-related TDP-43 encephalopathy, but we'll have time to discuss that in detail while you're here. In the meantime, the other members of the team are looking forward to meeting you."

And just like that, Gilbert and his wife whisked

Chloe away, the older man squiring his young colleague about as though she were his long-lost daughter.

After a stunned, silent moment as Sam and Kendrick watched this miracle unfold, Kendrick said, "She's a magician. Or a witch. Owens looks like pleased puss, while here I was, preparing to shield her from his frosty reception."

Sam just shook his head, not wanting to express his opinion, which was that not one man alive would be immune to Chloe. That would be far too revealing.

As though reading his thoughts, Kendrick rounded on Sam.

"Now, just how *briefly* did you two meet?"

"Oh, for goodness' sake." He gave his friend a narrow-eyed glare even while acknowledging he was just putting off the inevitable. They'd known each other almost their whole lives, and Kendrick wouldn't rest until he'd heard the entire story. "I'm going to get a drink."

There was no way he'd be getting into any of it with Kendrick tonight.

Not when he still had the entire evening to get through and the attraction he felt toward the British neurologist refused to wane the way he wanted it to.

CHAPTER FIVE

THE FIRST THREE weeks of Chloe's Jamaican adventure practically flew by, a blur of work and the type of social whirl she'd never been a part of before. Jamaicans, she realized, thrived on community and casually got together almost every evening after work for dinner or a couple of drinks before heading home. She'd been invited to the Owenses' home for dinner one night and to Kendrick and Rashida Mattison's a few more, where she'd met their two adorable children.

Rashida had also taken Chloe under her wing in a big way. As the owner of a marketing and special-events management company, she seemed to know everyone everywhere they went and had dragged Chloe along to meet up with friends a number of evenings.

Those evenings, along with a full schedule at the hospital, were probably why Chloe hadn't awakened just before her five-thirty alarm, as she usually did. And was also why she was still lying in her bed at five forty.

"Get up, lazybones," she told herself, before finding the impetus to push back the sheets and stick her feet over the edge.

But it still took far more energy than it should to actually sit up, and then a concerted effort to stand. Once in an upright position, she yawned and stretched her way into the bathroom, checking her watch to see how much time she had before her usual Wednesday-morning call with her gran.

At six on the dot, she was sitting on the little patio outside her living room with her cup of tea, connecting to her gran on her tablet via a video chat. The hills behind Kingston were just being touched by the golden glow of the rising sun, while the sky lightened from gray to silken blue.

"Hello darling." Her gran was smiling, and for some reason, seeing her like that made tears gather at the back of Chloe's eyes. "How was your week? Are you having a good time?"

"I've been run off my feet, but in the best possible way," she said, before explaining all she'd been up to. "Everyone has been so welcoming, and Christmas is already in the air, although there's still one week left in November. Some places already have their lights up, and I've been invited to a few parties."

"I don't doubt it," her gran said with a little

chuckle. "Christmas in Jamaica is always a big round of parties and jollification."

"Jollification? Not too sure I like the sound of that," Chloe teased. "But you know how much I love Christmas pudding, so that's something I'm really looking forward to."

Her gran chuckled. "I keep trying to tell you to learn how to make them yourself, but you won't listen."

"As long as I have you, you know I'm not going to bother to learn. Besides, I'm a disaster in the kitchen, as you well know."

They chatted for a little longer, and then Chloe had to hang up so as to get ready for work.

"Okay darling. Stay safe, and call me if you need anything at all," Gran said, as though Chloe were no more than twelve and away at summer camp. "I love you."

"I love you, too, Gran."

Silly to get teary-eyed again, and totally out of character really, but Chloe had to search out a tissue and wipe her cheeks.

"What on earth is wrong with me?" she groused, heading to the bathroom for her shower.

Then it struck her, like a blow to her solar plexus.

Frozen in place, she searched her memory.

She'd had her period just before going to San Francisco, hadn't she? Had she had one since then?

Galvanized, she stumbled over to the desk to

retrieve her day planner and started thumbing back through the pages. Her hands were shaking, and she had to pause constantly to make sure she'd checked each date.

By the time she found the notation about her period, she was forced to sit down on the nearest chair as her legs threatened to give out.

Mid-September.

That was the last time, although there was a cryptic notation about spotting in early October.

And it wasn't as though her periods were regular. That spotting could have been one, couldn't it? And yet, because of her endometriosis and the pain that was part and parcel of her menstrual cycle, it was normally easy to figure out.

Realizing she was on the verge of hyperventilating, she forced herself to take a couple deep breaths and think it through logically.

It was more likely that stress was the culprit rather than anything else. After the breakup with Finn, there'd been a couple of months where her cycle had been completely disrupted. Her gynecologist had assured her it was nothing to worry about, and after a while, things had returned to normal.

That was probably all there was to it.

The trip to San Francisco, divorce, then finding out about being chosen for the Kensington

Project were enough to throw even the staunch-est character off-kilter.

At least she knew it wasn't that she was preg-nant.

Even as her heart stuttered, she was shaking her head. The fertility specialist had been clear. With the scarring caused by the endometriosis being so severe, the chances of her becoming pregnant were slim to none. On top of that, the only time she'd been sexually active since Sep-tember was with Sam, and they'd used condoms.

No. It just wasn't possible, and she'd come to terms with her infertility a long time ago. Even thinking about pregnancy as an option would just open her up to more heartache, and she wouldn't go through the pain again. She'd always wanted children but had been forced to shelve that dream years before.

"No."

She said it aloud, the one strident word enough to shake her out of the state she'd been working herself into.

"Don't be stupid. Get up, get dressed and go to work."

And even though she got her legs working and went through her daily preparations, the nagging possibility wouldn't leave her mind.

So, on the way to work, she asked her driver, Delroy, to stop at a nearby pharmacy, and by lunchtime she had her answer.

Pregnant.

Impossible.

Yet, apparently not.

Her hands were shaking, the tester vibrating before her eyes so the plus sign wavered back and forth.

In fact, her entire body was vibrating, and a bubble of laughter tried to force its way up through her throat but couldn't get through. Realizing she was close to hysteria, she took a deep breath and the laughter, still trapped in her chest, caused her to hiccup. Putting a hand on her belly, she hunched over, fingers gently palpating the flesh as though trying to feel a difference.

Pregnant.

How?

Oh, she knew how, but not *how*. Had a condom broken? Had she and Sam slipped up in some way?

A wave of cold washed over her skin, freezing the laughter into trepidation.

Would Sam believe her when she told him she was pregnant, and that the baby was his?

Then she straightened and lifted her chin.

She didn't give a damn whether he did or didn't. *She* wanted this baby, desperately—wholeheartedly. And whatever decision he made about fatherhood was of no concern to her.

This was her chance to be a mother, and she wasn't just pleased, she was ecstatic, and no one—not Sam, or her family or friends—was going to make her feel otherwise.

Thus bolstered, she got a grip on her ragged and wildly swinging emotions and went to wash her face before assisting Dr. Owens in the clinic.

Sam finally started closing his patient's incision after a marathon surgery that had started mid-morning and gone all the way through to past three in the afternoon.

After being called up for the consult, and as the surgical team looked at the CT scan, Sam knew they were in for the long haul. Mr. Bogues had peritonitis, several large abscesses and what the radiologist agreed could be a fistula from complicated diverticulitis.

They'd gotten patient consent for the colon resection, and Sam had found someone to fill in for him at the afternoon clinic, then it was time to scrub in.

As the extent of the damage to the bowel, and the corresponding infection, was revealed, he marveled once more at his fellow human beings' capacity to withstand pain. Mr. Bogues must have been in constant agony for days, perhaps even a week, and if his wife hadn't insisted he go to the doctor that morning, he probably still would be.

By the time Mr. Bogues was in recovery and Sam had spoken to the patient's wife, it was gone four. As he walked back to his office, Sam's stomach grumbled, reminding him that break-fast—the only meal he'd had for the day—was far in the rearview mirror.

Closing his office door behind him, he checked his watch. He had time to write his report on the operation and then head up to the golf club for dominoes. Although there wouldn't be time to stop for anything to eat, it wasn't the first time he'd depended on the clubhouse kitchen for a meal.

Notes completed, he'd shut down his laptop and was putting it in the case when the phone on his desk rang.

"Dr. Powell here," he said mechanically, know-ing it would be his secretary.

"There's a Dr. Bailey here to see you. She's asking if you can spare her a few minutes."

He froze, his body going from calm to red-hot in an instant, his heart rate going into overdrive just at the sound of her name.

He'd avoided her, assiduously, for the last three weeks—turning down all invitations when he knew or suspected she'd be there too. But that hadn't stopped his memories from eroding his determination to keep her at arm's length.

It had taken strength of will he hadn't known he had just to stay away. Especially when there was a little voice inside saying it wouldn't hurt to check up on her, and make sure her stay was going well. Just passing by her office or her apartment, casually, would be no big deal, right?

But he didn't dare. He'd seen her in the distance—once walking with Dr. Owens, another time leaving for the day—and realized the pull she exerted over him was too strong. If he allowed it to become irresistible...

"Dr. Powell?"

He was so deep in his own head, his secretary's voice startled him.

He wanted to say he didn't have time to see Chloe, but his brain was too frazzled to come up with a good excuse as to why, so he said, "Send her in."

Busying himself with securing his computer in its bag, needing something to do with his hands, he barely allowed himself a quick upward glance when she entered the room. May as well have stared, though, as his desk, bag—everything—disappeared, replaced by Chloe's image, now seemingly seared into his retinas.

She had on beige pants and a light pink linen shirt, both of which fit her to perfection, highlighting the delicious curves of her figure. Her face was serious—there were two little creases between her eyebrows—which he'd come to learn were usually a precursor to one of her frowns.

"Thanks for seeing me," she said, her voice brisk. "I hope I'm not interrupting."

He risked another glance, unable to stop himself, and his already rushing pulse picked up additional speed as their gazes met.

She looked away first, glancing around the room, and he could breathe again.

"I'm actually just on my way out," he replied, before clearing his throat, hoping he'd sound normal as he continued, "Will this take long? Or can it wait until tomorrow? We could go to lunch, if you're free?"

That would give him time to prepare, to shore up his tenuous defenses. She'd looked back at him as he spoke, and the expression that fleetingly crossed her face, smoothing out the lines between her brows, confused him.

Was it relief?

"Er, of course," she said, turning right back around and heading for the door. "If that's more convenient."

Then she paused with her hand on the handle and briefly dropped her chin to her chest. Spinning on her heel, she faced him again.

"No, I'm sorry. I won't take much of your time, but I need to tell you something, and I'd rather just get it over with."

Walking to his consulting chair, she sat, placing her bag on her lap and hanging on to it as though it were a lifeline, her knuckles pale with the strain. Out of habit, once she was seated Sam pulled his chair out and sat, too, his gaze fixed on her face.

Chloe took a deep, audible breath and then said, "I'm pregnant."

The words made no sense to him. And yet they must have, because his heart stumbled and an icy pit opened up in his stomach. He tried to ask her to repeat what she'd said, but his larynx had seized, and when he opened his mouth, nothing came out.

"And before you ask, yes, the baby is yours. If it isn't, then we'll need to contact the Vatican about a miracle, because you're the only man I've been with since I left my husband two years ago."

Her words came at him as though from a distance. The frigid sensation had spread from his belly to form a band around his chest, causing the fleeting thought that perhaps he was having a myocardial infarction.

Then Chloe's face softened into an expression so beatific, all other thoughts flew from his head at the sight.

"It's actually a true miracle to me," she said, her voice low and so full of joy it melted the ice in his torso. "I was told I wasn't able to conceive because of endometriosis. So—" She paused, her chin tilting up to that pugnacious angle he'd come to know so well. "So what I wanted you to know is that I'm keeping this baby, and if you don't want to be involved in his or her life, I can assure you my child will lack for nothing."

He knew he should say something, but try as

he might, nothing came out. And it felt as though he'd been turned to stone. No, to some kind of gelatinous substance that precluded movement, so all he could do was watch as Chloe gave him a small smile and stood up.

"I'll let you get on with your afternoon," she said, and then she was gone.

Pregnant? With my child?

Sam's brain couldn't seem to grasp the concept, and he finally staggered to his feet, not knowing where exactly he planned to go.

Endometriosis...

His heart stopped, and a wave of nausea had him swallowing against the thickness rising in his throat.

Chloe's pregnancy was high-risk.

His legs gave way again, and he plopped back into his chair, momentarily overcome by fear so strong it dulled the edges of his sight to darkness.

What would be worse, he wondered dully: losing a child you never knew existed until it was gone or a second one you suddenly realized you wanted almost too much?

Because, just then, Sam realized the baby growing in Chloe Bailey's womb meant more to him than he'd have ever expected.

That baby—*his child*—was as much a miracle for him as it was for its mother.

CHAPTER SIX

Chloe wasn't sure how she'd made it through the day, and even after speaking to Sam, a fog of disbelief still clouded her brain.

After getting back to the apartment, she closed the door behind her with a sigh and wandered straight through the living room and out onto the balcony. The entire day she'd felt unable to catch her breath, and now, as she lowered herself into a chair, she exhaled hard, searching for equilibrium.

Pregnant.

Tears of joy filled her eyes, causing the scene below to blur into a fantastical kaleidoscope as the reality slammed home again.

She'd been told conception wasn't possible—nor even probable. This was, indeed, a miracle, and she was determined to do everything she could to carry her baby to term.

But first she had to pull herself together so as to think it all through.

What she'd told Sam was true. If he didn't want

to be a part of their child's life, that was fine. Hurtful, yes, but still fine. It wasn't as though they'd had a grand love affair or made promises to each other. When you got right down to it, they hardly knew each other at all, except in the most basic, physical way. She'd think him a heel if he abandoned his own flesh and blood, but not everyone was cut out for parenthood. Some people even actively avoided it, for whatever reason.

If he were one of those, then it was probably better he not be involved. Sometimes a reluctant parent was worse than one who never even tried.

Besides, they lived in different countries, a couple thousand-or-more miles apart. Logistically, it wouldn't be easy maintaining a relationship when he was in Jamaica and the child was in England.

England.

That brought her to another point she hadn't considered yet: Would she be endangering her child by staying in Jamaica for the full two months? Should she go home right away and seek a medical consultation with her ob-gyn?

While she'd never walked away from any assignment in her life, she'd do it in a heartbeat if it would be best for her baby.

Best to ask her doctor. Dr. Abdul would advise her as to the best course of action.

Chloe got up, glad there was something constructive she could do, and was crossing the living room for her phone when she remembered it would be going on eleven at night in London.

Pausing, she shook her head at her own nonsense. Hopefully this muddle-headedness wouldn't be a constant during her pregnancy. She'd call first thing in the morning.

She was about to go and change into something more comfortable when her phone rang and the doorbell sounded, simultaneously. Her phone was on the dining table, and she grabbed it as she made her way to look out through the peephole.

"Hi, Rashida. How are you?"

When a glance into the passageway showed a stern-faced Sam standing out there, whatever Rashida said got lost in the buzzing sound filling her ears. Chloe stepped back, as though Sam could see her, and tightened her grip on her phone.

Taking a deep breath, she willed herself to calm. Reaching for the handle to unlock the door, she strove for a breezy, unconcerned tone.

"I'm sorry, Rashida, but you faded out there for a moment. Could you repeat that, please?"

Chloe pulled the door open as Rashida replied, "I said I'm heading to Mayfair Hotel to meet up with some friends and I'll be passing your place in a little while, if you wanted to come."

Waving Sam in with a casual hand, Chloe turned away, leaving him to close the door.

"Sorry, I can't tonight. I have some paperwork to catch up on, but thanks for the invite."

"Aw, okay. Maybe tomorrow evening? If not, you're definitely coming out to Maiden Cay with us on Sunday. There's a session out there—a sort of pre-Christmas bash—and Kendrick's brother is taking us out there on his boat."

Sam hadn't moved from his spot just inside the door. Chloe could see him in the glass front of the dining room buffet. It gave her a little more time to gather her defenses.

"I'll let you know," she told Rashida, torn between reluctance to get off the phone and a kind of terrifying anticipation of what Sam had to say.

"All right. Talk to you tomorrow."

"Bye," Chloe said, hearing the trepidation in her own voice but tilting her chin up as she ended the call.

Turning toward Sam, she raised her brows but didn't speak, waiting to hear what he had to say. His eyes were hidden behind dark glasses, but she saw him swallow, hard, before he spoke.

"You didn't give me a chance to say anything before you left my office."

It was obvious he was striving for an even tone, but all she heard was accusation, and her hackles rose.

"I thought you'd like a bit of time to think about what I said without me sitting there, staring at you."

Sam sighed, rubbing his chin. The rasp of his hand over stubble had a shiver running down Chloe's spine.

She knew, with breath-stealing clarity, exactly what it felt like to have that stubble against her skin.

Suddenly her perfectly adequate flat was too small—too close with Sam in it—and she spun away, saying, "Let's talk out on the balcony."

They settled at the table outside, and it felt too small, as well. Sam took off his dark glasses, and the distance between them seemed to shrink even farther. This close she could see his shifting expressions, the firmness of his lips and the tightness at the corner of his eyes. Those indications of stress heightened her own tension, and she twisted her fingers together beneath the table, where he wouldn't see.

She was still waiting for him to break the silence, refusing to say anything first. As far as she was concerned, she'd said what she needed to. It was his turn.

Instead of speaking immediately, he reached into the pocket of his white bush jacket and pulled out a slip of paper, which he slid across the table toward her.

"I made an appointment for you to see Dr. Millicent Hall. She's the best obstetrician I know, and when I explained your situation, she agreed to fit you in tomorrow evening. She suggested you ask your gynecologist to forward your records so she can see how bad your endometriosis is."

Chloe sat back, staring at him. Anger rippled through her, and although she tried to tamp it down, her voice came out higher than usual.

"You what?"

Sam's eyes narrowed. "Why do you sound upset? You need to see a doctor."

"You do realize I am a doctor, don't you?"

"A neurologist. Not an obstetrician."

"Listen." She leaned forward and jabbed a finger toward him. "If things had gone as we planned, you wouldn't even be aware of this baby, and that would have been fine. I'm perfectly capable of taking care of myself *and* my child."

Sam's eyes sparked, and his fingers, which had been flat on the table, curled to form fists. His mouth opened...and then closed again as he let out a long, loud exhale through his nose. His expression flashed from anger to pain and then smoothed into a calm, severe mask.

"You say you're pregnant with my child yet seem to expect that I'll just stand back and not try to do the right thing. That's not how this is going to work. So get used to it."

She drew in a breath, ready to fire back, but Sam held up his hand.

"If you want to, you can tell people what's going on and ask for advice as to which obstetrician to go to, but I'm telling you, everyone who's in the know will tell you to go to Millie. She's the best there is. There is the added bonus of her not working at Kingston General, so if you're hoping to keep your condition secret, she'd be a better bet than, say, Dr. Maynard."

Chloe was going to say she didn't care who knew she was pregnant, but bit back the words.

It was probably Sam who cared whether people knew about it or not, and if she was in a reasonable frame of mind, she'd understand why.

No one knew they'd slept together, and he was probably worried about how it would look should any of his friends find out.

"I'm not concerned about secrecy," she told him, making her opinion of his high-handedness clear by the sharpness of her tone. "But my plan is to contact my doctor in the morning and ask for her professional opinion as to whether I should return home immediately or if I can continue with the project. I'm not saying I *won't* see a doctor here, if my doctor says I can stay, but those are arrangements I'm quite capable of making myself."

Sam leaned back in his chair, his gaze boring into hers for what seemed like an eternity, lingering until she felt that familiar—and unwanted—tightening in her belly, and heat rose up into her face.

Suddenly he shook his head and asked, "Have you eaten yet?"

Surprised by the change of subject, Chloe replied, "No. I just got home and haven't given supper any thought."

"I haven't eaten since breakfast," he confessed. "I was in surgery since before noon."

Funny how just then she could see his weariness, when before all she had seen was sternness and strength. She felt herself softening, even as she tried to hold on to her annoyance at his autocratic behavior.

"And I can't be reasonable on an empty stomach," he continued, the corners of his mouth lifting slightly. "Come and have dinner with me, and then we can talk some more."

It was on the tip of her tongue to refuse. Everything about Sam Powell shrieked "danger." But she had to admit, if only just to herself, that his acceptance of what she'd told him about being pregnant with his baby was more than she'd had any right to expect. And his wanting to take responsibility, even if the way he was going about it got her back up, forced her to view him in a rather better light.

But was it wise to spend more time with him than was strictly necessary? How close did they really have to be to effectively coparent, especially long distance?

She sighed to herself. Those were questions that needed to be worked out, and pushing him away at this stage just meant putting off the inevitable.

She stood up.

"Okay. Give me a few minutes, and then we can go."

The look of relief on his face was unmistakable, and he smiled, causing Chloe's heart to stumble over itself.

"Great."

Quickly hustling inside to freshen up, Chloe tried to remind herself they had business to discuss: important issues regarding their child.

Looking at her reflection in the mirror, she gave herself a stern talking-to. All there was between them was one night of passion, and the new life they'd created. Nothing more.

When Chloe went inside, Sam let out a harsh breath and scrubbed at his cheek.

Why was she being so difficult when he was trying to do the right thing by their child—and her? What did Chloe see that made her so hostile to the idea of him being involved with her pregnancy?

What had Vicky seen that had made her hide the fact she was carrying his child all those years ago?

The memory of Chloe saying that if things had gone the way they'd originally planned, he wouldn't even know about her pregnancy speared right through him. That certainly hadn't been his plan eight years ago with Vicky. They'd been together for almost three years and had spoken, albeit in vague terms, about spending their lives together. He'd have thought she'd tell him she was pregnant as soon as she knew. Instead, she'd used the fact they were based in different cities—her busy with her doctorate in Philadelphia, him doing his residency in Baltimore—to hide her condition.

Once more the irony of Vicky's ghost inadvertently bringing Sam and Chloe together made him shake his head.

It had been the anniversary of Vicky's death when he'd first seen Chloe, and after noticing how gorgeous she was, he'd seen her pensive expression. The downturned lips and lines between her brows. The pain in her eyes and restless confusion in the way she twisted her glass back and forth.

Although he couldn't say how, in her, he'd recognized a kindred spirit—another soul who'd been hurt by forces outside their control.

He'd been longing for some type of forgetfulness despite knowing it was something he'd never truly achieve. Away from home, he didn't have to pretend the day held no significance. In San Francisco he could spend the evening without anyone asking him what was wrong.

No one would care.

And it was strangely soothing to know he wasn't alone in the darkness of his mood, for there, in the same room, was someone else seemingly wrestling with a similar agony.

Even as he'd thought it, he'd seen Chloe's expression go through a slow but glorious transformation. From sad, she'd grown thoughtful, and then she'd smiled as though suddenly finding a way to cast aside whatever had caused her sorrow and to emerge into the light of a new day.

He'd wanted that.

Wanted her.

For succor and to hopefully somehow find a path back to happiness through her, if just for that one night.

And she'd given him all he'd dreamed of, and more.

For the first time in a long time—if ever—he'd lost himself in a woman's arms. It had not just been an erotic feast but an almost spiritual experience. In Chloe he'd found the forgetting he'd craved, along with an ecstasy he hadn't expected and, as he fell asleep, hadn't been sure he knew how to process.

When he'd awoken in the morning and found her gone, he'd been surprised at his own disappointment and anger. Over the next days and weeks, he'd been intent on telling himself none of it mattered.

That it had been wonderful but was over, and that was for the best.

Now here he was, back in her presence and tied to her through the life she carried in her belly. A life he could hardly bear to think about and yet couldn't stop thinking about.

This was a second chance. Not with Chloe—he had no interest in giving his heart to any woman—but to be the father he hadn't been able to be before.

And no one—not Chloe, not even he, himself—was going to stop him from doing what needed to be done to protect this precious new life.

"I'm ready."

Lost in his torturous thoughts, he hadn't heard her approach and looked up, still dazed, to see she'd changed out of her work clothes. Instead of the tailored outfit she'd had on, she was wearing white capris and a floral blouse that beautifully showcased her curvy figure.

How would she look, round and bountiful with his child?

Desire, white-hot and unmistakable, cracked like lightning through his flesh, leaving him shaken.

There was no time for that—no place for it between them anymore.

So he forced it aside and rose, aware of her careful perusal. The caution in her gaze. He didn't smile, just nodded and waved toward the front door.

"Let's go."

When she turned away, he let out a silent breath before sweeping the piece of paper with the information about her appointment into his hand.

Whether Chloe knew it or not, or liked it or not, she'd be going.

Sam would make sure of it.

CHAPTER SEVEN

WHEN CHLOE EXPRESSED no preference as to where she wanted to eat, Sam took her to a small Chinese restaurant where, although the place itself was not much to look at, the food was amazing.

"Why is it that the Chinese food in Jamaica is so darn good?" she asked Sam, only half joking. It really was delicious.

He gave her a small smile. "My understanding is that most of the Chinese immigrants to Jamaica came from the Hakka region of China, and the food they popularized here differs from the more widespread Cantonese and Sichuan. Of course, the dash of Jamaican spice doesn't hurt."

"Whatever the reason, it's fabulous."

They'd kept the conversation light, as though skirting around the minefield of her pregnancy, and Sam seemed determined not to talk about any of it until he'd eaten.

"Have you tried Jamaican food since you got here?"

Chloe couldn't help chuckling. "I grew up eat-ing Jamaican food. My dad's parents are Jamaican."

His brows lowered slightly. "I didn't know that."

She shrugged. "Not surprising, really."

Sam's eyes narrowed, and Chloe braced for whatever was coming next, but all he asked was, "So, what's your favorite meal?"

"Gosh, I don't know," she said, looking down at her plate. Whenever their eyes met, a shiver of desire traveled along her skin, and keeping that kind of response to a minimum was imperative. "Maybe oxtail and rice and peas. Or stew peas."

"Did you get mackerel rundown?"

Chloe smiled and nodded, swallowing what she had in her mouth before replying, "That was Granddad's favorite, so we usually had it on his birthday. But you know what I'm really looking forward to?" Sam's eyebrows rose in response to her question, so she told him, "Christmas pudding. I love it, and this year, I get to taste more than just my Gran's."

His lips curved into a teasing smile, and the corners of his eyes crinkled. This time she couldn't seem to tear her gaze away.

"So, you have a sweet tooth."

"I do." No use denying it, and she found herself smiling back at Sam. "I try to keep it under control, though."

His gaze slid briefly down, then snapped back

up to meet hers. "Looks to me like you're doing a good job."

There it was again: that tingling rush of interest firing along her spine and settling, warm and arousing, in her stomach. Her heart was racing, and gooseflesh shivered across her back and down her arms.

Mouth suddenly dry, she dragged her tongue across her lower lip and saw his eyelids droop as his eyes tracked the motion.

Then he blinked and focused on the dish of pork and *muknee* on the table, breaking the spell.

And when he next spoke, it was to ask how she was getting on at the hospital, throwing a veneer of casualness over the tension that continued to shimmer in the air between them.

"It's going really well, I think. I've been seeing patients as well as doing informal training sessions with both the neurologists and the nurses in the department. Dr. Owens is very interested in a study we've been doing about the efficacy of already available drugs on certain symptoms of Alzheimer's disease and other forms of dementia. If they're able to prescribe drugs that already have generic variants, it can cut costs and make treatment more readily available for some of the patients. He's even asked me to take the evening clinic next week." She smiled down at her plate. "I think I've passed his test, and he's feeling a bit better about having me here."

"I think it's safe to say you were in from your welcome dinner. Kendrick and I saw you melt the ice right from the word *go*."

The little glow of satisfaction his words brought was ridiculous but unmistakable, and Chloe had to remind herself not to get caught back up in Sam's charm. She'd been down that road before and look where it had got her!

Not that she was complaining about being pregnant. Far from it. She was eternally grateful for the blessing. Yet it was coming home to her that she was now tied to this man forever, and she wasn't at all sure how she felt about that part of the equation.

"Do you have a particular area of neurology you specialize in?"

His curiosity seemed benign enough, so she didn't hesitate to answer.

"Most of the research I've been involved in leans toward unraveling the mysteries of dementia, but when it comes to patients, I treat all kinds of neurological disorders and diseases. Which is why Dr. Owens seems comfortable with me taking over the clinic for the evening. Apparently, his wife's receiving an award and he doesn't want to take the chance that the clinic runs late and he misses the ceremony."

"I don't blame him," Sam said, shaking his head and using his chopsticks to spear the last steamed dumpling. "That's the life of a doctor, isn't it? We have to be completely reliable when it comes to work but are often the worst when it comes to being available in our private lives."

Was that a warning, that although he was claiming to want to be involved in their child's life, she shouldn't count on him to be committed to raising him or her?

The question rose to the tip of her tongue and was bitten back.

She'd file that away for future consideration.

When they left the restaurant, the sun had set, and Chloe lifted her face to catch a little of the cooling breeze and smiled to herself.

"What's so funny?" Sam asked, having opened her car door so she could get in.

"Oh, just thinking about my family and friends back in London who are probably digging out their jumpers and carrying their macs and umbrellas wherever they go. And here I am wearing capris and a sleeveless top."

"Just wait until the Christmas breeze starts blowing." Sam chuckled, leaning on the door, his face alight with mischief. "Then you'll see Jamaicans bundled up like they're in the Arctic."

She couldn't help joining his laughter. It wasn't so much what he'd said but his expression. The twinkling eyes. A little bit of a wrinkling of his nose. That glorious smile, which did crazy things to her insides and caused the overwhelming urge to tug his face down so she could kiss him.

Thankfully, before she had a chance to turn thought into deed, he closed her door and, still smiling, walked around to get into the driver's seat.

"Are you in a rush to get home?" he asked, as he settled into his seat.

"Not really," she replied, before thinking it through. Then, in case he got the wrong idea, she added, "But I'm sure you have somewhere else to be."

"No, I don't," he assured her with far more intensity than she was expecting as he put the car in gear.

Where they ended up was Devon House, a heritage site that had been pointed out to her but Chloe hadn't visited yet.

"Oh, how stunning," she said, as they drove onto the grounds and she got a close-up view of the stately home. The trees and mansion were decorated with lights, and pots of poinsettias in full bloom had been dotted everywhere. "So festive."

"You like Christmas?"

"Usually," she replied, not wanting to get into why she wasn't as enthusiastic as she used to be. "I like decorating and gift giving, but of course this year will be very different."

"Without your family?"

"Mmm-hmm. And just being here rather than

home in London. I'm just not sure what it'll look like."

He nodded as he put the vehicle in park. "It was a while back, but I remember my first Christmas away from Jamaica, when I was at school in the States. Definitely a bit disorienting."

"You didn't come home on break?"

They opened their doors and got out, then he replied.

"My parents couldn't afford to have me flying back and forth for the shorter breaks, so I stayed there most years and just came back for summers if I didn't have any courses planned. A couple of years, Kendrick and I spent Christmas together, but usually I was alone or with other classmates whose celebrations were very different from what I was used to."

"Where did you go to school?" she asked, as she followed him into the redbrick courtyard where various shops were housed.

"Maryland," he replied, naming a well-known university in that state.

"Winter there must have been a rude awakening after Jamaica."

"Oh, it was, believe me. For a while, I was considering staying in the US after my residency, but evenings like this make me glad I didn't."

She could see why. Pausing beneath the branches of a tree, she turned in a small circle, taking in the well-maintained buildings, the shops all aglow and decorated with bows, ornaments and the ubiquitous poinsettias in the windows. The air was warm but not sultry—perfect for sitting outside and enjoying the evening.

"Now comes the hard choice," he said, his voice so serious she spun around to face him, her heart giving a little leap of fear. But even before he spoke again, she saw the twinkle in his eyes, and her sudden spurt of trepidation waned. "Ice cream or baked goods?"

"Oh," she said, on a little gasp of relief. "Definitely ice cream."

"Girl after my own heart," he said, resting his hand lightly on the small of her back to guide her toward the store and leaving a tingling hotspot when he let go. "Take a look at the menu, so you know what you want when you get to the front of the line."

She chose a cup with two scoops—one fruit basket, the other sorrel, which she'd never realized could be used for ice cream, although she'd had the drink at Christmas. Sam got Devon Stout in a cone, and once they'd received their treats, they wandered out into the garden and sat on a bench.

"Do you know the history of this house?"

Chloe had to admit she didn't.

"It was built in the late 1800s by George Steibel, reputed to be Jamaica's first Black millionaire. He was a shipping magnate, and it's said that he could see all the way down to the harbor from the window at the very top of the house and would watch his ships come in. They've renovated the house and give tours, but it's too late to do one now. You'd have to come during the day."

"I think I will," she said, before taking a taste of her ice cream and giving a happy hum as the tropical flavors exploded on her tongue. "This is so good."

Sam shifted beside her, and a glance in his direction found him staring at her in a way that had heat trickling down her spine.

They both looked away at the same time.

It came to her then, just how dangerous this entire situation had become.

On first meeting Sam, it had been all about the physical attraction and the thrill of a tryst with a stranger, far from the prying eyes of anyone who knew her. Afterward for Chloe, the memory of Sam had taken on an almost mythical eroticism. She'd never see him again, and so it was safe to think about him. Fantasize about that night. Even imagine what other days—and nights—would be like with him.

Now, with her pregnancy, they were being forced to get to know each other on a totally different level. There could be no effective coparenting if they chose to remain strangers.

Not that the initial erotic interest had waned, at least on her part, but it had to take a back seat.

There was no room for the kind of complications having even a short-term affair would bring, and no matter what, she wouldn't let herself even think of getting back into Sam's bed.

Sexual gratification was nowhere as important as her child's future relationship with its father, and it was up to Chloe to make sure nothing arose to jeopardize it.

And although she was enjoying this companionable interlude, there was one issue she needed to address, to make sure it didn't loom sometime in the future and cause problems.

Bracing herself, Chloe said, "You seem very calm about this entire situation. I'm actually surprised at how readily you've accepted the pregnancy."

Sam paused with his cone almost to his lips and then lowered it with a sigh. She wasn't surprised when his other hand came up and he rubbed his palm along his jawline to his chin. That seemed to be his reaction whenever he was tense or was taking a moment to think.

Finally, he replied, "Honestly, my first thought was to question it all. Whether you really were pregnant and, if you were, whether the baby was mine. I won't lie and tell you that none of the usual responses popped into my head. 'We used condoms.' 'How do I know she's telling the truth?'"

Sam paused, and Chloe realized she'd been

holding her breath. Letting it out silently, she found the courage to ask, "So, what do you think now? I mean, I can understand if you want a paternity test after the baby is born—"

He stopped the flow of her words with an uplifted hand.

"Actually, I believe you."

There was no reason for his admission to make her smile. It wasn't approbation to be told someone thought you were telling the truth when you were, but somehow hearing it felt that way.

"Thank you."

He shook his head. "I saw the genuine happiness in your face when you called it a miracle, and realized you really were prepared to have and raise the child by yourself. In my mind, that means you have no reason to lie to me. In fact, you could have just kept the pregnancy to yourself and not bothered to even tell me about it. I'd be none the wiser, once you left Jamaica and went back home."

The thought shocked her, and she blurted, "I wouldn't do that. It wouldn't be right."

The look he gave her was unfathomable.

"Wouldn't it?"

"No. If we'd not met again, and I discovered the pregnancy without knowing your last name or where to find you, that would be one thing. But to know where you were and not tell you? That would be unfair to you and to our child too."

Sam nodded slowly but didn't reply, and Chloe wondered what the expression was that flashed through his eyes.

She could have sworn it was pain, but why would what she'd said be hurtful?

Finally, Sam said, "Listen, I know we don't know each other very well, but I think we should at least try to be friends."

"I agree," she replied, trying to sound firm and confident when she was anything but. "That will make it easier going forward."

"That's my way of thinking too. But I need you to realize that when I make suggestions, I'm doing so in your best interests—and the baby's too."

She knew where this was heading, and tried to sidestep. "I'm sure that's so, but I have a right to make my own decisions. It's not as though I'm without medical experience, so we're even on that front."

Sam let out a long breath through his nose and nodded, although there was that hand again, scraping back and forth across his chin.

"True, and I'll never try to say otherwise. Neither of us is an obstetrician, after all, but I'd personally feel better if you're under medical care while you're here."

Oh, she so wanted to argue, to say it was *her* body and *her* baby and she knew best.

Yet although the former was true, the latter really wasn't.

Sam had stepped up and accepted his responsibility far more readily than she'd had a right to expect, and if she shut him out now, it might make things more difficult in the future. And although neither of them had said it aloud, her pregnancy was high-risk. It really was in the baby's best interest that she see a qualified physician sooner rather than later.

"All right," she reluctantly agreed. "I'll go to the appointment tomorrow."

"Excellent." At least he had the good sense not to sound as though he was gloating as he took the piece of paper out of his pocket and handed it to her. "I'll pick you up at six thirty."

"I don't need—"

The look he sent her way had the rest of the sentence drying up in her throat.

"Six thirty."

CHAPTER EIGHT

DR. HALL TURNED out to be a matronly woman with kind eyes and the type of brisk, no-nonsense approach that Chloe appreciated. Besides a quick upward twitch of her brows when Chloe indicated Sam could come into the office, Millicent Hall had no questions about his involvement. Although she obviously knew Sam well, she treated them both with complete professionalism.

Earlier in the day her nurse had called Chloe to say the doctor had sent an order for blood tests to a lab independent of Kingston General, and Chloe had stopped there before work. After Dr. Hall examined Chloe and they were all sitting at her desk, she pulled a folder closer to her and placed her hands atop it.

"I've had a chance to look at the records Dr. Abdul sent, as well as your bloodwork, and to this point everything appears to be fine. Since there's nothing an ultrasound can tell me about the reduction or changes to your lesions, I think we'll wait to do one at your next visit."

Sam shifted, leaning forward to place his elbows on his knees, obviously intent on what Dr. Hall was saying although her comments were addressed to Chloe. It was silly to feel a little disappointed not to have the chance to see the baby via ultrasound, and Chloe simply nodded in agreement.

"But as you no doubt know, your endometriosis puts your pregnancy into the high-risk category. Dr. Abdul has classified your endometriosis as between levels two and three, and is worried there could be complications caused by your lesions. This means you'll need careful prenatal monitoring and to be on the watch for any signs of problems, not just in your first trimester."

It was what Chloe had expected to hear, but even so, her heart sank.

Sam reached over and took her hand, giving her fingers a squeeze.

The coldness of his fingers took her by surprise, and a quick glance his way showed tightness at the corners of his mouth and eyes.

She squeezed back, and he rubbed his thumb across her knuckles. Somehow, that soft brush of skin on skin calmed her, easing her tension and giving her a warm spurt of pleasure.

"We also have to be on the watch for placenta previa and preeclampsia. Some studies seem to indicate the risk of placenta previa is heightened in women who, like you, had surgical treatment for their endometriosis. And while it's not sure there is a correlation between endometriosis and gestational diabetes, you have other risk factors, as well."

Sam's hand seemed even colder than before, and another glance had Chloe thinking he looked positively gray.

"What can we do to minimize the risks?" he asked, his voice little better than a low rumble.

"Unfortunately, not a lot," Dr. Hall replied, her tone conveying her sympathy. "However, Chloe will need to get ample rest, limit overexertion—both professionally and while exercising—and making sure she eats a fiber-rich diet."

The sound Sam made conveyed something akin to disbelief, which was backed up by his asking, "That's it? There's nothing else that can be done?"

"Just all the usual things pregnant women who want a healthy gestation and birth do," Dr. Hall briskly repeated, then blithely went on to outline those, ending up with, "And there's no reason to forego sexual activity, as long as there is no pain on penetration."

Sam dropped her hand as though suddenly stung. Chloe couldn't help noticing that before he let her fingers go, his had warmed considerably.

After Dr. Hall gave Chloe some pamphlets and additional instructions, including an appointment in two weeks' time, they took their leave and walked back out to Sam's vehicle.

"Have you eaten yet?" he asked, as he opened her door for her.

"I had something when I got home," she replied, doing her best not to touch him as she got into the vehicle. Something about that tender moment when he'd reached for her hand threatened to melt her resolve not to get any further entangled with him.

He closed her door without replying, but when he got into the driver's seat, he said, "Okay, good. I did, too, but there are some things you and I need to discuss. Do you mind going somewhere where we can talk?"

It was on the tip of her tongue to plead weariness, but instead she sighed silently and said, "Okay."

It wasn't that she didn't want to spend more time in his company. On the contrary, she was eager to spend as much time with him as she could and knew she must be a little crazy to even feel that way. Better to get away posthaste, so she could give herself the stern lecture she so obviously needed, but it was too late for that now.

Instead of heading back toward New Kingston, Sam drove north.

"What are you up to this weekend?" he asked, his tone casual.

"I'm not sure yet." She leaned her head back

against the seat and looked out the passenger window. Not really in the mood for small talk, she reminded herself to be glad he hadn't plunged right into whatever it was he wanted to discuss so urgently. "I usually take care of chores on Saturday, and Rashida invited me to go out on Kendrick's brother's boat to some island or the other."

"Maiden Cay. They have parties out there periodically, and I guess everyone is ramping up for Christmas, hence them having one so late in the year." He seemed to hesitate for a moment and then said, "They invited me too."

Now it was her turn to pause, trying to figure out exactly what he was trying to say.

"Do you want me to refuse the invitation?"

After all, Kendrick, Rashida and Sam had all been friends long before she came along.

"No, why should you?" He sounded genuinely confused. "Marlon's boat is big enough to handle it if the sea gets rough, so you won't get bounced around too much. You don't get seasick, do you? That would be my only worry, since it could lead to dehydration."

"No, I don't." Silly to feel once more gratified by his concern. "Do you think you'll be going?"

"Yeah, man. Sure. It's always a good time."

It was on the tip of her tongue to say she'd found it strange he'd never been around any of the times she'd hung out with Kendrick and Rashida, but she bit back the words. There was no need to maybe get him thinking she'd been disappointed—which she had been.

They were traveling along a road she recognized, and Sam confirmed it by pointing and saying, "That leads to where Kendrick and Rashida live."

As he said it, a car raced toward them on their side of the road, narrowly missing Sam's vehicle as it tucked in behind another vehicle to avoid a head-on collision. Chloe clutched the armrest on the door and pressed an imaginary brake pedal, suppressing a squeak of surprise. When she looked back over her shoulder, it was to see the car swerve back into the wrong lane and speed off again.

Sam threw her an amused glance.

"It's okay. I promise not to get into an accident."

"I don't know how you avoid one, with the way people drive. I thought about renting a car when I first got here, but honestly, I don't know how you do it."

He actually chuckled. "You get used to it, especially when you've grown up here, but yeah, it can be a hair-raising experience."

They were passing a shopping center, and the hills, which always seemed like a backdrop to the city, were suddenly right there. Sam turned off the main road, and they were immediately climbing, driving past houses built right onto the hillside on one side and below the level of the road on the other.

Sam touched a button on the rearview mirror, and Chloe saw a pair of wrought-iron gates start to open just ahead.

When he turned into the driveway, she asked, "Where are we?"

"My home," he said calmly, hitting the button again to close the gates behind them. "We can talk here without anyone interrupting us."

Why did she always feel as though she wanted to object whenever he said or did anything unexpected? It really wasn't like her—at least not the her she was familiar with—but something about his bossiness really was aggravating.

So when he drove into the garage, Chloe made no effort to get out of the car. When he came around and opened her door, she sat looking up at him for a long beat.

Sam looked back, seemingly unconcerned.

"Aren't you getting out? Or would you prefer to sit here while I go inside?"

Chloe huffed but swung her legs out of the vehicle and stepped down. "It would have been nice if you'd told me where we were going and *asked* if I was comfortable with it."

She would have moved past him, but Sam was blocking her way, his solid form suddenly too close, the warmth and scent of maleness suddenly too potent.

"I'm sorry," he said, and there was no hint of sarcasm in the quiet words. "I really am. I'm… so used to just doing whatever I want to, it didn't even occur to me you might object. If you don't feel safe—"

"Don't be silly." Why did he always make her feel wrong-footed? "If I didn't feel safe with you, I'd have never…"

And just like that, it was there between them. The night in San Francisco. The passion. Ecstasy.

Sam felt it too. It was obvious from the way his eyelids drooped and his mouth softened. They were close. Way too close. Yet Chloe couldn't find the strength to step back.

Instead, what she wanted to do was step forward into his arms. Lose herself once more in his kisses. His lovemaking.

But there was no room in her life for that kind of forgetting. Not anymore. With a baby to consider, she had to be smart and keep Sam at a distance so their relationship wouldn't mess up life going forward.

As though the same thought occurred to him, Sam stepped back, and Chloe could breathe freely again.

"Come on in," he said, as though that fraught moment had never happened, leaving Chloe wondering if she'd imagined it. But her nerves were all a-jangle, and the slam of the car door made her jump.

His home was multilevel, built into the side of the hill like its neighbors. After turning off the alarm system via a panel by the garage door, Sam bypassed the rooms on the ground floor and led Chloe up a short flight of stairs to the living room. As she hovered near the top of the steps, Sam crossed the room to pull back the curtains, revealing a stunning view of the city spread out below. After he opened the sliding glass door, letting in a cooling breeze, Chloe walked over and they both stepped outside.

Leaning against the balcony railing, she said, "How lovely. Seeing the city from this angle is amazing. Can you see the sea from here?"

"Way in the distance, with the Palisadoes Peninsula just a smudge on the horizon." He turned so he was facing her, but Chloe kept her gaze glued to the view. She hadn't fully recovered from the moment in the garage and didn't trust herself not to get drawn in by his magnetism again. "And it's not quite as nice a view on hazy days. Can I get you something to drink? Limeade or soda or water?"

"No. I'm fine, thank you."

She'd been dreading hearing whatever it was he wanted to talk about, but now wished he'd just get on with it. Being so close, knowing they were alone was doing insane things to her equilibrium.

"I've been thinking…"

Chloe didn't like the way his voice trailed off like that, and her heart rate went into double time at the slowly drawled words. Yet she didn't respond, just waited for him to go on.

"You should move in here with me, for the rest of your trip."

Sam kept his gaze trained on Chloe's profile, waiting for her to react to his words. It took her so long to do so, he was beginning to think she was planning on ignoring what he'd said, then she shook her head.

"No."

"You'll be more comfortable here. I have a lady who comes in to cook and clean three days a week, so you'll never have to worry about any of that. And, because we both work at Kingston General, I can drive you back and forth each day, without any issues."

She turned and looked at him then, her dark eyes searching his face.

Of course, the main reason was so he could keep an eye on her and make sure everything was going well. Be there for her if…

His mind shied away from that thought, just as Chloe shook her head again.

"No, thank you."

He couldn't take no for an answer. The emotions that had overtaken him as he'd listened to

Millie Hall describe the risks inherent in Chloe's pregnancy demanded he do something—anything—to mitigate the chance of miscarriage. Having her here would allow him to keep a firm eye on her—make sure she ate properly, didn't work longer hours than necessary or take on more than she should.

Yet he knew saying those things wouldn't go over well with her, and as he struggled to find the right arguments to win her over, she lifted a hand.

"I can see you getting ready to ride roughshod over me," she said in a surprisingly gentle tone. "But it won't work. I have no intention of letting anyone—not even my family—know about this baby until I'm reasonably sure…"

He saw it then, as it flashed through her eyes. The same fear he battled with. Without thinking it through, he reached for her and gathered her close.

She resisted, her body tense and stiff for a long moment, and then she relaxed, almost melting against him as her arms went around his waist.

Burying his face in her hair, he said, "We'll get through this, Chloe. Everything will work out."

"Unfortunately, the outcome really isn't in our hands," she replied softly.

"No, but we can be in it together and support each other for as long as you're here." He was trying so hard to ignore the way she felt in his arms—the sweet weight of her resting against him. The way they fit so perfectly. The moment was tender, and beautiful. Too special to let his outrageous desire destroy. "I know it's unconventional. Maybe some people will think it scandalous. But we're adults, and that shouldn't matter."

She leaned back slightly so as to meet his gaze, and in the dim light from the living room, her expression seemed to shift with varied emotions, one following the other. And then she inhaled so deeply he felt her breasts lift against his chest in what could only be an accidental caress but one that struck additional fire into his belly.

"I don't want to think right now, Sam. Don't want to search for answers. It feels too overwhelming and confusing. I just need simplicity—and something I'm absolutely sure of."

And with that, she raised her arms to loop around his neck, and pulled his lips down to meet hers.

CHAPTER NINE

CHLOE HAD SPOKEN the unvarnished truth.

She didn't want to think anymore. Not with all the turmoil rushing through her head, and the sensations bombarding her from being in Sam's arms.

Somehow, feeling—actual physical closeness—was suddenly more important.

In Sam's lovemaking could be found sweet forgetfulness and perhaps even a kind of clarity.

Yet those thoughts dissolved into nothingness under the onslaught of Sam's kisses, which left her weak-kneed and breathless with desire.

Oh, she knew the risks—to herself and her equilibrium—but his tenderness and acceptance had been her undoing.

Now she wanted his touch. Wanted to once more feel like the woman only he had ever moved her to be. Strong. Demanding. In control, until with a burst of pleasure, control was lost, leaving satiation behind.

Sam's breathing was as rushed as hers, and his

hands roamed—restless and arousing—over her back and arms and bottom, pulling her impossibly closer with each hard caress.

And, oh, how he could kiss.

His mouth moved on hers, urging her to open for him, to let their tongues dance against each other in sexy, provocative play. There was restrained ferocity in the way he kissed, and it drove Chloe wild.

Worming her arms between their bodies, she unbuttoned his shirt, baring his muscular chest to her roving palms. He was already in the process of returning the favor, and Chloe shivered as the cool night air touched her overheated skin when he pushed her top down her arms. It didn't take any coaxing at all for her to allow him to pull it off, and it sagged around her waist.

And still they kissed.

There were things she wanted to tell him— like how her nipples ached for his fingers or his mouth. Or how wet he would find her when he finally got her pants off.

These were things she'd never said to a man before. Not until that night in San Francisco, when inhibitions had fallen away as though they'd never existed.

Sam brought out the sexual being that had been trapped inside her all her life, and the freedom of letting go was more potent than tequila.

His mouth left hers only to latch on to her

neck, and the sound she made was harsh with carnal pleasure.

"Yes," she said, arching her head back so as to give him access. "There. Oh…" They both groaned at the same time, and Chloe heard herself say, "You make me want to come, just from that."

A growl broke from Sam's throat and he picked her up. As she wrapped her legs around his waist, he turned to carry her back inside. The hard length of his erection resting right between her legs made her squirm, and she rubbed against it, feeling the tension in her belly tightening. Tightening.

"Dammit, Chloe." He lowered her to the couch, and she spread her thighs, pulling him down on top of her. "You make me wild. I feel like a teenager again when you do things like that."

She would have laughed if she'd had the breath for it, but the need she felt had put her on a mission that demanded satisfaction.

"I don't want to wait, Sam. You make me feel better than I've ever felt before. Give me what I need."

He levered up to kneel between her legs, and the expression on his face had a hard shudder firing down her spine. It was the look of a man on the edge—feral, dangerous, aroused. Yet although he moved quickly, he was also surprisingly gentle as he removed the rest of her clothes until she lay bare and wanton before him.

Then, despite her egging him on, telling him to hurry, he shook his head.

"No," he said, taking her foot in his hand and kissing her ankle. "I *won't* hurry. We have all night."

"Take off your pants," she demanded, but he only laughed and shook his head.

"Not yet." He shifted slightly away when she tried to reach his fly herself. "You're so impatient."

By way of reply, since she couldn't do as she wanted and he was taking his own sweet time, she cupped her own breasts and pinched the nipples.

"God, yes," he growled. "Pinch them again. I love how responsive they are."

"I want you to do it." She pouted. "You should be touching them with your hands or mouth."

"I'm getting there," he replied, before kissing her calf.

"But so slowly," she said, before her voice was lost in a low gasp as he lifted her leg higher and his tongue swiped behind her knee.

And she'd been so intent on what his mouth was doing, she didn't realize his other hand had slid up and rested on her inner thigh until his thumb parted her folds, sending a shockwave through her system.

She cried out, arching her hips to deepen the contact, and Sam didn't disappoint. His knowing touch circled and pressed, enticing her arousal to a feverish peak until she came almost silently, no breath left for sound.

"There," he said, his voice deep and dark, almost dreamy. It made her shudder, not just from the timbre but also from the way his breath rushed across her thigh. "Was that enough?"

Opening her eyes, she realized he'd slipped off the couch and was kneeling beside it. Somehow, in the midst of her orgasm, he'd maneuvered her body over, so one leg was still on the cushion while the other was draped over his shoulder.

"No, it wasn't enough," she rasped, her throat tight, her body already craving another endorphin jolt from his loving.

"Tell me what you want," he said, his eyes gleaming behind slumberous lids, his lips soft, slightly upturned and seductive. "I love how you know what you want and how to ask for it."

So she did, her voice getting higher and more strained as his mouth and tongue, hot and slick against her flesh, took her over the edge once more.

Sam didn't give Chloe much time to come down off her orgasmic high before he surged to his feet and held out his hand.

"Come," he said, hardly able to get the word

out through the tightness of his throat. "Upstairs. I want you in my bed."

She rose, her legs wobbly, and he steadied her when she swayed before turning her toward the corner of the room and the staircase leading up to the bedrooms.

He was behind her as she climbed, and he couldn't keep his hands off her, so much so that when she reached the landing, he stepped up behind her, and pulled her back against his chest.

Her breasts were glorious weights in his hands, and when he found her nipples—tightly puckered—with his fingers, he reveled in her soft moan of delight.

Chloe made him crazy with need, but at the same time, he wanted this to last as long as he could. If she touched him right now, if he entered her body, he'd be done.

Done, done, done.

So he leaned against the wall, putting off the moment when they'd be on his bed together.

"Sam." Her voice was little more than a breath. "Oh, Sam. What are you doing to me?"

Loving you.

The thought ricocheted in his brain, but he didn't say it, just kept caressing her, teasing her, until she shivered in his arms, her hips rotating against his groin.

"Now, Sam," she said, her voice tight. "I can't wait."

Although he was touching her, his fingers slipping through folds so wet and hot he could hardly stand it, coaxing her toward another orgasm, he knew what she was asking.

And he couldn't resist.

Reluctantly moving his hands until they rested on her hips, he nudged her up the last four steps to the corridor above.

"Last door on the right."

He hardly recognized his own voice. It came out like the rasp of a file over wood, rough and raw.

When he walked into his room behind her and turned on the light, there was a moment where his heart, which had been pounding, slowed and then missed a beat. He faltered, unsure what the sensation making him light-headed could be. Then Chloe climbed into his bed and everything fell into place.

He followed, stopping to kick off his footwear and then remove his pants. The entire time he was watching her—seeing the restless way her fingers moved, the slow, sexy smile that tilted her luscious lips.

She held out her arms to him, and he didn't hesitate. Climbing in beside her, he pulled her close and kissed her over and over again, needing the closeness almost more than the physical satisfaction he knew awaited.

Habit had him reaching for a condom, respect

for her had him putting it on, although there was nothing he wanted more than to be bareback inside her tight, wet heat.

Pulling her against his side, he said, "You drive, Chloe," and the look of sheer, sensual delight she gave him made him harder, if that was humanly possible.

She straddled his thighs and then, as though savoring every second, slowly slid home.

Sam screwed his eyes shut, fighting the need to move, thrust, to give in to the orgasm already building.

But this was Chloe's show, and he tried his best to let her have her way.

She chose a slow, rocking motion that had his breath coming fast and heavy and took his control to the breaking point.

Yet she cried out first, as her hips suddenly picked up speed, her inner muscles contracting. Her orgasm took him over the edge so quickly, and with such intensity, an involuntary shout broke from his throat.

She collapsed down across his chest, and then after a few minutes where they both struggled with their breathing, she rolled to his side.

Sam floated, satiated and pleasure-drunk, sleep dragging at his eyelids. He tried to fight it, but when he looked down at Chloe, he realized she'd already dozed off and he allowed himself to follow suit.

"Sam. Sam."

Her voice called to him and he instinctively tightened his grip, keeping her flush against his chest. Even half-asleep he knew if he let her go, she would disappear again.

"Sam. Wake up."

A sharp jab to his ribs from a well-placed elbow brought him fully awake.

"Huh? What?"

"I need to go to the lav. And you need to take me home."

Loosening his arms from around her was a lot harder than it should have been, but Sam forced himself to do it, then watched as she made her way to the en suite bathroom. With a huge yawn, Sam rolled over and dragged his pillow into a more comfortable position.

When Chloe came out, she poked him.

"Come on, Sam. It's late, and I need to get back to my flat."

"Why don't you just stay here, and I'll take you home early in the morning."

"Nope. I'm sorry, but that won't work."

"All right," he grumbled, before rolling over and grabbing her to pull her back down on top of him. "All right."

She melted into him, just for a moment, and then she wriggled free.

"None of that, my lad. Up you get."

So, under duress, he complied when what he

really wanted was for her to climb back into bed and go back to sleep in his arms.

Driving her home, the car was quiet except for the radio, both of them seemingly lost in thought. At her apartment, he walked her to her door and gently kissed her good-night.

"I meant what I said earlier," he told her. "I want you to move in with me."

The sweet, satisfied expression fell from her face, and those little lines between her brows came back.

"That's not a good idea, Sam, irrespective of what happened this evening. I'm not ready to have people knowing about the baby, and if I move in with you, there'll be questions I don't want to answer."

It seemed so obvious to him, and Sam saw her words as an opening rather than a firm refusal.

"We're going to have to answer those questions eventually, especially after the baby is born. It'll be easier for us to explain if it's clear we're involved from now on, rather than it looking as though we were just sneaking around."

"I'm not moving in with you, Sam." She eased out of his embrace, leaving him with an empty sensation. Leaning against her doorjamb, she gave him a level look. "This situation is complicated enough without compounding it."

"Think about it," he said, making it a demand when he was inclined to plead. "Please. I want to introduce you to my family, let them get to know you while you're here. It would go a long way to making things easier in the long run."

"We can do that without us living together," she pointed out, those frown lines coming and going. "I just don't want…"

When her voice faded, he asked, "What? What don't you want?"

She took a deep breath and then sighed before facing him again, her eyes wide and luminous. "I don't want either of us to get in too deep. I just got out of a marriage that left me questioning everything about myself—my life, expectations, reactions. I don't think I trust myself to remain objective, especially with the added fact of being pregnant."

He heard the honesty in her tone and wondered if he should match it. Yet did she really need to know about Vicky? And even if she did, it wasn't a conversation for one o'clock in the morning while standing outside her door.

"I hear what you're saying, but I think it would work out to our advantage, so promise me you'll think about it anyway?"

"Yeah. I will," she said with what sounded like a healthy dose of irony in her voice. "'Night, Sam."

After she'd gone inside and closed the door behind her, Sam stood there for a moment lost in thought, before heading back to the elevator.

He wished he could say he knew neither of them were in any danger of catching feelings, but he was honest enough with himself to admit Chloe had a valid point. The last thing he wanted was to get too emotionally involved, despite the fact she was carrying his child. Chloe seemed to feel the same way, too, worrying that she might find herself in the kind of rebound situation that's hard to make proper sense of or get out of.

No, he definitely wasn't interested in forever, but if he could get her to agree to spending the rest of her time in Jamaica with him, he couldn't see how it could be a bad thing. Everyone would know they'd had a relationship, so the baby wouldn't come as a huge shock.

Plus, he thought as he got back into his car, he'd have the wonderful pleasure of having her in his bed every night, without having to drive her home in the wee hours of the morning.

And that would more than make up for any other risks!

CHAPTER TEN

How she was able to refuse Sam's suggestion that she move in with him was a mystery to Chloe, and she was still shaking her head over that the next morning. And while prepping for morning rounds, only half of her brain was on the workday ahead. The other was still wrestling with the question of *why* she'd said no.

It wasn't as though she hadn't wanted to say an enthusiastic yes. That had been her first impulse. Why shouldn't they enjoy themselves together for the next six or so weeks? They were both single adults, and it would, as he'd pointed out, make explaining her pregnancy to friends and family easier.

Plus after the night before, she was ravenous to get back into his bed.

No matter what, she couldn't bring herself to regret one moment of Sam's lovemaking. There was something about the way he touched her that made her feel like a princess.

No, a queen. Imperious and powerful, demanding her due and getting it.

That was heady stuff.

However, she had another problem.

Sam scared her. A lot.

There was something so compelling and forceful about her reactions to him, she knew it really wouldn't be hard to become attached. A one-night stand was all well and good, but living in his house, sleeping in his bed every night knowing full well the relationship wasn't going anywhere? She wasn't at all sure she was capable of pulling that off and keeping her heart intact, especially since she was carrying his child.

Surely it was better to play it safe? Keeping her own space, seeing him only on her own terms might help her maintain an emotional distance. There was no reason why they couldn't enjoy sex without her actually living with him.

"Dr. Bailey?" Nurse Oliver put her head around Chloe's office door. "Dr. Pullar from psychiatrics sent up for a consult. Dr. Owens is asking you to go."

Thankful for the distraction, Chloe got directions to the psychiatric unit and went on her way. Yet as she made her way across the hospital grounds to the other wing, her thoughts circled right back to the pickle she was in.

Nothing seemed clear-cut to her anymore,

leaving her wondering how to figure out if whatever decisions she made were right.

The reality was her experiences with men were limited. Her only real relationship had been with Finn, and she'd fallen for him so hard and so fast that by the time she'd regained her senses, she was walking down the aisle.

Only in hindsight did she realize that in many ways she'd been subsumed by him and their relationship. Although she knew herself to be a competent, modern woman, they'd never really had a partnership. Finn made demands and decisions, and she'd marched in lockstep along with him, sometimes against her better judgement. It was no excuse to say she'd done that to keep the peace or because he'd go and do whatever he wanted to anyway.

It just made her a twit.

She'd always been the peacemaker of the family, smoothing ruffled feathers and keeping things on track, and Finn—knowing that—had taken advantage. Worst of all, she'd let him.

Who's to say Sam wasn't cut from the same cloth?

He'd said himself that he was used to getting his own way and doing whatever he wanted without thought for anyone else. While he'd shown her consideration in many ways, he'd also been overbearing in others.

She wasn't up for that type of ride again, even

temporarily—thank you very much—so getting emotionally tangled up with Sam wasn't on.

"Nice to meet you," Dr. Pullar said, after Chloe had found the correct area and introduced herself. While escorting her toward the examination room, he continued, "Is it unusual for you to get a call from a psychiatrist wanting a consult?"

"Not at all," she replied, sending him a smile. "We're very big on cooperative medicine at Royal Kensington, so whatever specialty is needed becomes a part of the patient's team. I'm guessing it's the same here."

"It is," he replied, opening a door and waving her through. "Especially when we get referrals and the patient hasn't been under consistent medical care, as is the case with Ms. Barnes."

Twenty-five-year-old Kadisha Barnes had been taken to a rural hospital by a family member. According to the history they'd gathered there, she'd started to display personality changes a few months before, including extreme mood swings, which had gradually increased. She'd resisted going to the doctor, for reasons best described as paranoid. They'd taken her to the nearest hospital the day before, after she'd suffered extreme confusion and then had a seizure.

"As is sometimes the case because it's difficult to get all the tests done outside the larger centers, she was referred to us for psychiatric evaluation, but I'd like your opinion."

As Chloe took the file from him, she asked, "You suspect physiological disease rather than psychiatric?"

"Yes, from the progression."

Looking at the notes, Chloe could understand why the psychiatrist might think so. Off the top of her head, Chloe could name a number of diseases that mimicked the effects of psychiatric disorders and had to be ruled out before a diagnosis could be made.

"Did the family member list any other changes they may have noticed recently, or has Ms. Barnes been able to answer any questions?"

Calvin Pullar shook his head. "Unfortunately, the history I've given you in the notes is all we have, and Ms. Barnes is frightened and won't speak."

"Have you examined her yet?"

He shook his head. "She's truly terrified, and I decided it would be better to get you down here first rather than putting her through repeated examinations."

"Sensible. Let's take a look."

Kadisha was indeed scared, but there was less of an adverse reaction when Chloe and the female nurse spoke to her, while she shrank back when Dr. Pullar approached, so Chloe took the lead. Although she wouldn't answer questions, Kadisha did follow directions, allowing Chloe to come to a tentative diagnosis.

"I'd suggest both TSH and T3 blood tests," she told Dr. Pullar. "Although there's no sign of a goiter, I highly suspect hyperthyroidism."

He nodded, and thanked her for her time. "I'll call up later and let you know the results."

As she made her way back toward her office, of course Sam Powell wormed his way back into her thoughts, and her blood heated anew as she thought about the night before.

The memories made it hard to think straight and be realistic. How easy it would be to just give in to the desire, without worrying about the consequences. While acknowledging it was best to keep on a friendly footing with him so they could be cordial and pleasant going forward, there could be such a thing as *too* friendly.

Or, more like too *invested*.

She sighed, trying to be logical. Only after the pregnancy revelation had Sam come near her. Didn't that indicate his main interest was the baby, no matter what else happened between them?

With a sigh, Chloe acknowledged to herself that she was in danger of getting in way over her head. What she needed was to cultivate detachment, so it would be easier to walk away when the time came.

Just as she was about to exit the building, as though her thoughts had conjured him, she heard Sam call her name, and her heart leaped. With her hand still on the door, she watched him stride toward her and only just stopped herself from grinning like a fool in response to his obvious pleasure at seeing her.

"What are you doing on this side of the hospital?" he asked, as he came alongside her and reached out to open the door for her.

"Just examining a patient. Psych asked for a consult," she replied, stepping out into the courtyard and welcoming the wave of heat since she was sure her face was glowing. She knew she should tell him there was no need to accompany her back, but somehow the words wouldn't come out.

"So, how're you this morning?" he asked, as they set off toward the other side of the compound.

"I'm well, thank you," she replied demurely, even though gooseflesh broke out across her shoulders, and her nipples peaked at his intimate tone. So much for detachment! "And you?"

The sound he made was somewhere between a snort and a chuckle. "As well as can be expected, when I spent most of the rest of the night thinking about you."

There went her heart again, jumping and racing like a crazy thing.

"Sam—"

She tried for a quelling tone and apparently succeeded, because Sam laughed.

"Hey, don't go all schoolmarm on me. I'm just speaking the truth. I was wondering… Do you have any plans about seeing other parts of the island while you're here?"

The change in subject surprised her and she paused, looking up at him as she replied, "Yes, but I'm not sure where to go, or how to get there yet. I haven't given it as much thought as I should."

"Okay, let's work something out, and I'll take you."

"You don't have to—"

"I know, but I want to. It would be a shame for you to come this far and not see some of the island. Where were your grandparents from?"

"Well, Granddad was born in Portland, and Granny is from Hanover."

He chuckled. "Of course. Opposite ends of the island. Well, let me see what I can come up with, okay? What about this evening? Are you doing anything?"

She started walking again, trying to quell the rush of excitement she felt just from talking to him. The man was a menace to her equilibrium, and she forced an airy tone into her voice, trying not to let him see just how off-kilter she was in his presence.

"Oh, I don't know. Rashida usually calls in the afternoon to make plans. She also said she wants to take me shopping on Saturday, and then I'm supposed to spend the night with them and go to Maiden Cay on Sunday."

There was no way to accurately interpret the sound he made, and Chloe wasn't going to ask what it meant.

"Well, if she doesn't call for you to go out with her, want to have dinner with me this evening?"

They were approaching the entrance, and she slowed just a bit while trying to figure out how to respond. Of course she wanted to see him, but hadn't she just been telling herself it was imperative to maintain some sort of distance? That couldn't happen if she were constantly in his company.

Finally, she shook her head. "No, thank you. I have a full clinic load today and I think I'll just go home and relax."

"Well, you'll have to eat anyway. I could bring something over and—"

"Listen," she said firmly, giving him a stern look and stopping far enough away from the doors so they wouldn't be overheard. "You don't need to feel as though you have to take care of me or entertain me, Sam. I'm more than capable of doing that myself, okay? I'll see you on Sunday, for the boat ride."

And then, because she stupidly felt like crying, she turned on her heel and marched to the

door, determined to put her mind back on work
and forget all about Sam Powell.

At least for a while.

Sam wasn't sure what to make of Chloe's cool,
cutting response to a simple invitation to dinner,
and his first impulse was to follow her back into
the hospital and get her to explain. After the night
they'd spent together, he really hadn't expected
her to brush him off like that.

Not that he'd thought she'd be suddenly head
over heels for him, either, nor did he want her to
be. He remembered all too well the way she'd
slipped out of his life in San Francisco. Clearly,
Chloe Bailey was a master at compartmentaliz-
ing and keeping her emotions firmly in check,
no matter what she might say to the contrary.

It made him wonder exactly what it was her ex-
husband had done, and if whatever it was were
to blame for the way she was handling Sam now.
That was something else he'd like to corner her
and ask her about.

But instead of going after her, he turned and
headed back over to the other building. Although
it irked him to not demand an explanation, having grown up with sisters and seen how his parents dealt with arguments, he decided to leave
her alone for at least the rest of the day.

Not that she'd sounded angry, Sam thought
as he headed back to his office. Maybe she was

just a bit overwhelmed by everything and needed some space. Everyone handled situations differently, and just because he was itching to have it out with her didn't mean he had the right to demand that conversation.

Perhaps she was even doubtful of his motivations, both for sleeping with her and for asking her to come and stay with him, and that made her overcautious.

In truth, Sam was a little muddled about his motivations himself, so while he chafed at the decision not to contact Chloe Friday afternoon, it seemed for the best. It might give him a chance to figure out what, exactly, he was doing.

The evening found him uncharacteristically alone at home, leaning on the veranda railing, looking out at the city lights. Usually he'd be out somewhere, playing darts or having a couple of drinks since he wasn't on call, but tonight he wasn't up for it.

It wasn't in his nature to unburden himself to others or look for someone else to solve his problems. He'd always handled his business himself. Even after Vicky died, the only person he'd spoken to about her pregnancy was Kendrick, who was his oldest friend. More like a brother, really. In Sam's eyes, there'd been no need to make his parents sadder than they had already been or open himself up to a new, more dreadful level of pity.

Chloe, at least, had told him about the baby immediately, and he had to give her credit for that. She'd also advised him that, realistically, they didn't need him, which was something he both knew was true and resented.

The thought came to him then that not only did he want this baby but he *wanted* to be needed— to be an indispensable part of, if not Chloe's life, then his child's.

Did he have a right to be? Did he deserve that kind of grace?

He'd questioned his fitness to be a father many times since Vicky's death. If she hadn't doubted his abilities to parent, why hadn't she told him about their baby? It was, to him, the only thing that made any sense, no matter how many other reasons Kendrick espoused.

Are you sure the baby was yours?

Maybe she didn't plan on keeping it?

Strange how now those questions brought only a dull ache and a lingering wish to know rather than the grinding anguish they always had before. He'd acknowledged he'd never know the answers—that whatever he thought or suspected would remain conjecture—but this sensation, so much like acceptance, was new.

As new and as unexpected as his overwhelming pleasure at knowing he was going to be a father.

Why he felt so strongly about Chloe's pregnancy, he didn't know and didn't feel the need to dwell on too deeply. He preferred to act rather than navel-gaze.

Taking a sip of his drink, he tried to be logical about what absolutely needed to be done.

With the way things stood, Chloe would be on the island only until the end of the year. After that, she'd return to the UK.

Everything inside was telling him this thing between them needed to be settled, and soon.

Long before she was scheduled to return to London.

She'd turned him down flat when he'd asked her to move in with him, even temporarily, but maybe there was some way to change her mind—other than making love to her until she was too tired to go home?

If he could prove he was someone she could count on to think about what she wanted, who would provide whatever she and their child needed, would that be enough?

For some reason he couldn't shake the idea that if he could just get her to move in with him, it wouldn't be too hard to get her to agree to stay on the island past January first.

Maybe…

His brain faltered, not wanting to think too deeply about marriage. He'd planned on marrying Vicky—had trusted her in a way he'd never been able to trust another woman after discovering her duplicity. When she died, he'd pledged not to get entangled—not to risk himself in that way—again.

Yet fate had presented him with an opportunity he hadn't wanted but couldn't turn away from, and he needed to make sure he didn't blow it.

And if taking care of his child properly meant marrying a woman he desired but didn't love, was he willing to go that far?

Perhaps if he only desired her, it wouldn't be enough, but Sam had to admit he genuinely liked Chloe. He'd go so far as to say she was intriguing, infuriating and enticing. He admired her intelligence and drive along with her dedication to her profession.

And he wanted her physically, with an intensity that often approached the point of pain. If last night was any indication, the passion between them hadn't subsided one iota. If anything, it had heightened to explosive proportions.

Many a marriage had been successfully based on far less. There was no reason to believe they couldn't make a good lasting go of it, especially to protect and properly raise their child together.

But, even *if* he got comfortable with the idea, Sam realized it would make no sense to think about broaching it with Chloe. She'd had no problem shooting him down over something as inconsequential as dinner. No doubt she'd blow him out of the water if he just came right out and said they should get married.

No. He needed a plan. One that would show her the type of man he truly was and convince her they were meant to be together, for the sake of their child.

And he didn't have a heck of a lot of time to think one up and put it into play.

The days were ticking away a lot faster than he'd like. Soon it would be December, and there would be only a month before she was set to leave.

Whatever he needed to do had to be done soon, before he lost the chance completely.

CHAPTER ELEVEN

CHLOE SPENT FRIDAY evening alone and out of sorts as Rashida had taken her children to a birthday party. Grumpy and annoyed with herself for it, she'd sat down to watch a documentary in the evening and fallen asleep, awakening at minutes to midnight.

The nap hadn't refreshed her, though, so she went straight to bed, only to awaken in the morning before the sun was even up, although she usually slept in a little on the weekends. At least she had texts from Cora, complaining about a man she was working with in Sweden, to occupy her, and chatting back and forth helped her spirits. Something about the way Cora mentioned Jonas had Chloe wondering what she wasn't saying… but who was she to pry? Here she was, pregnant by a man she hadn't even told her best friend about and saying nary a word.

The invitation to go shopping with Rashida that morning didn't materialize, either, as her son had a stomachache and needed attention.

That, of course, was perfectly understandable, but Chloe then spent a few hours sulking while taking care of chores. Finally, tired of her own nonsense, she sat down to read up on new research results, sent to her by the team at Royal Kensington, and promptly fell asleep—again. Awakening sometime later, she sat for a moment, disoriented, wondering what exactly had roused her, and it was only when the doorbell sounded again that she came to completely.

Was this the infamous pregnancy-induced tiredness she'd always heard about? If so, she thought as she stumbled to the door, it rather sucked.

When she looked through the peephole to find Sam on her doorstep, she was instantly fully awake and ready for battle.

In fact, if she were being strictly honest, she'd been ready for battle since their last conversation, expecting Sam either to call her back or try to see her to have it out. He'd taken the wind out of her sails by the simple method of ignoring her, while she'd stewed on both the fact they'd slept together again and that he'd asked her to go stay with him.

Which, in turn, just made her even madder.

So she yanked open the door with a certain level of ferocity, but whatever she'd planned to say died in her throat when she saw the jumble of bags and boxes in the corridor.

Finally, she gestured to them and said, "What on earth is all this?"

"Christmas decorations," he said, picking up a long box in one hand and a couple of bags in the other. "You said you liked putting them up, and I thought you were probably missing doing that this year, so I brought you some."

She was too shocked to do anything but move out of his way as he headed into the apartment.

"That wasn't necessary…"

He put down his burdens and gave her a grin before heading back out the door for the rest.

"No, but some of the best things in life aren't strictly necessary, are they? I just figured that since you'd be here for Christmas, it would be nice for your place to be festive."

"But why?" She was still standing beside the open door like a ninny, watching him stride back and forth with boxes and bags. Had he bought out an entire Christmas store? Did they even have stores like that in Jamaica? "I'll just have to take it all down before I leave on the first of January."

"I'll help you," he replied, shoving the last couple of boxes into the apartment with his foot, then closing the door behind him. "Besides, it's the Christmas season. You might want to invite people over or take pictures to send to your family back in the UK. Would you want the place to be bare?"

"I wouldn't care," she said, unaccountably both annoyed and close to crying, unable to figure out if he were being nice or somehow manipulative. "It's too much bother."

He'd stooped to start opening the box clearly marked Christmas Tree, but paused to rock back on his heels and look up at her.

"I've upset you." Rising to his feet, he shook his head. "I'm sorry. That certainly wasn't my intent. I can take all of this stuff away if you really don't want it."

Now he was making her feel like an ungrateful cow, and Chloe blinked, trying to hold back her stupid tears.

"It's not that I don't want it, it just seems like a lot of trouble to go to when it'll all just have to come back down in a few weeks."

"Bah," he said. "It's not a big deal at all. Please don't cry."

"I'm not crying," she huffed, even though he'd dissolved into a watery silhouette because of the moisture in her eyes. "I don't cry."

She saw him move but wasn't fully prepared when he gathered her close. The immediate jolt of electricity through her system miraculously had her tears drying up, and for a moment, she fought the urge to relax and take the comfort his embrace offered. But her body hadn't got the memo and went almost boneless, even as it heated and tingled, remembering all the amazingly naughty things they'd done two nights before.

"Of course you don't cry," he agreed. "Although I have heard that pregnant women sometimes do things they've never done before—like burst into tears or, in Rashida's case, be nice to their husbands."

Chloe's huff of laughter at his remark about the oft-acerbic Rashida turned into a hiccup.

"You're terrible," she said, sniffling, trying not to pay attention to how wonderful it felt to have his arms around her and determined not to let him know how close she was to dragging him off to her bed. "And I'm sorry. Although it doesn't excuse my grouchiness, I've been up since five this morning."

Sam leaned back so he could see her face, his palms making soothing circles on her back. At least, she assumed they were supposed to be soothing instead of making her blood start rushing through her veins. "Have you eaten?"

"What is it with you and food?" she asked, forcing a little chuckle and trying to ease away from his far-too-tempting body. "You're constantly trying to feed me."

Tightening his grip so she couldn't get away without a struggle, he tilted his head to one side as though thinking about it. Finally, he replied, "I love to eat, to be honest, so since it's important to me, I guess I figure it is to everyone else, too, and I try to feed the people I care about. I guess food is my love language."

Oh, she wasn't putting even a toe into *that* water, so Chloe fell back on answering his initial question.

"I had something when I got up."

"That was a long time ago, so let's go get something to eat, and then you can let me know whether I should get all this stuff out of your place or whether we're going to decorate."

In the final analysis, it was easier to agree than to argue, but it was also a little scary to realize just how seeing Sam improved her mood.

As she went to change her clothes, Chloe firmly reminded herself how far she'd come since her divorce and how strong she had to be to protect herself and her baby from future disappointments.

Despite the sparks of desire still firing across her skin from being in Sam's embrace, it wouldn't do to keep falling into his arms—and his bed.

She needed to keep their relationship as simple as possible, no matter how difficult that might be with his sexy smiles and mind-destroying lovemaking. If all he wanted was to keep her sweet, so as to make things run smoother in the future, there were other ways to make it happen which didn't include losing herself in the process.

All she had to do was keep reminding herself of that fact.

* * *

Sam took Chloe to the Liguanea Club, which served delicious food. And since she'd been upset before, which had made his heart ache, he also made sure to keep the conversation light.

Well, as light as possible when you have two doctors chatting together, trying not to bring up the very subjects foremost on their minds.

Like babies. And wanting to sleep together again. And what their relationship should look like going forward—a subject that insisted on taking up far more space in his head than Sam liked, but that wouldn't be dismissed.

"It's stupid, I know," Chloe said, as she spread her napkin on her lap, preparing to tuck in to a plate of *escovitch* fish, mackerel rundown and ackee cooked with salt pork, accompanied by *bammy* and a boiled dumpling. "But I've been extremely surprised at the variety of diseases I've treated since I've been here. I expected the usual ones, like epilepsy and dementia, but I've already seen a number of cases of myasthenia gravis and even one poor young man with a rare one—Alice in Wonderland syndrome."

"What?" Sam was intrigued. "I've never even heard of that."

"I've only ever seen one other patient with it," Chloe admitted, as she cut a bite of fish. "And that was unfortunately caused by a brain tumor. But none of the tests we did on the youngster I saw last week have come back positive, so it seems to be a chronic case with no treatment available. I just hope his mother believed me when I told her it should eventually subside. He's only eleven, and usually these cases resolve themselves within a few years."

"Wait, start at the beginning. What is Alice in Wonderland syndrome anyway?"

She chewed and swallowed before answering.

"It usually manifests as an alteration of visual perception—you know, like Alice saw, where she or things around her got big or small—although there can also be hallucinations and time distortions. With the altered visual perception, objects and even body parts can appear smaller or larger than they actually are. But it isn't permanent. It comes and goes. So for instance, in the young man's case, he suddenly thought his hands had swollen to three times their normal size. When it first happened, he called out for his mother, thinking something was wrong with him, but when she came into the room, he thought her head was swollen too."

"That's frankly terrifying," Sam admitted. "He must have been frightened out of his wits."

"He was," Chloe said, shaking her head. "As was his mother. She told her neighbor, and eventually it got back to the pastor of her church, and he said the child was possessed by demons. They spent who-knows-how-long trying to pray him well before the mother realized he wasn't getting better and took him to the children's hospital. They referred him to Kingston General."

Sam nodded. "I've had a few patients that have come to me only after the prayers didn't work, too, but I'll admit never for something like that. I almost don't blame them for thinking there was something supernatural about it."

She smiled, and Sam realized it was the first time she'd done so freely that day. Seeing it made him feel lighter somehow, as though a weight he hadn't even noticed he was carrying had eased off his shoulders.

"It's one of the stranger neurological disorders, and it's often experienced by people with very specific diseases, like brain tumors, Epstein-Barr, temporal-lobe epilepsy and migraines. When I was reading up on it again, I also found a recorded case of a man with the degenerative brain disease, Creutzfeldt-Jakob, who'd experienced the visual symptoms."

"You said there's no treatment?"

"In his case, I advised against any. There were no signs of underlying conditions that would bring it on, and so, in reality, I had nothing to treat. It took a good deal of time getting his mother to understand that there was no magic pill and even longer to convince the little fellow that no, he wasn't insane nor demon-possessed and eventually it would stop."

Sam shook his head. "Save me from the patient that thinks I'm a magician and one wave of my magic scalpel or pill dispenser will change everything. I have a lady I've operated on twice already for pica. The first time, we saw from her scans that she had a mass in her stomach and feared cancer. It was hair. I removed it and told her she needs to go to the psychiatrist. She asked if there wasn't 'something I could give her' to help her stop. I told her the psychiatrist might be able to, but I couldn't. A year later, she was back."

"Did she ever go to get therapy?"

"I hope so, since I haven't seen her after her final post-op examination, but it wouldn't surprise me if I see her turn up again."

To his surprise, Chloe's eyes started to twinkle, and she laughed. "You realize that if the people at the next table were to hear us talking, it might completely put them off their food, right?"

Sam couldn't help laughing with her.

"You're right. I remember the looks we used to get in fast-food joints when all of us med students would hang out, especially after anatomy class. We even had people get up and leave."

"I'm not surprised. I remember those days well."

Then he turned the conversation to her family, learning that she was the eldest of four, that her maternal grandfather, who suffered from early-onset dementia was still alive but now in a nursing home, and that she was closest to her paternal grandmother.

"She was always strict about how we behaved and carried ourselves but never tried to tell us how to live our lives, if that makes sense?"

"It does. My mother's a lot like that. Which reminds me—every year she has a charity gala and I'd really like it if you'd come with me."

His heart sank as those two little lines between her brows made an appearance.

"I don't think that's appropriate, Sam. All your family will be there, won't they? They'll have questions if they see us together."

The urge to tell her she was now a part of his family was so strong, it took all his control not to say anything.

Where was that even coming from?

Instead, he shrugged as though he didn't care one way or the other and said, "I told you I wanted to introduce you to them, and it would be easier having them all in one place. Besides, it'll be a crowd of people, so it's not like a private family-only affair. Kendrick and Rashida will be there too."

Chloe didn't look convinced. "I'll think about it. When is it?"

"December fourth. She always says it's the kickoff to the Christmas season, and none of us have the heart to tell her anything different. This year's been hard on her, though. She needs hip-replacement surgery, but they're trying to get her to lose some weight first. Sometimes I think she's not following the dietician's plan as a way to put off the operation."

Man, he was trying to keep it all light, but the sight of those lines between her brows was stressing him out.

He hadn't realized how important it was for him to introduce her to his family until she didn't seem to want it, and now he was forced to act as though it was no problem.

She would, he thought as he jabbed his fork into his fish, make him crazy if he wasn't careful.

But maybe she already had, and he just hadn't cottoned on to that fact yet?

That thought made him smile, and he looked up to find her staring at him.

The lines had smoothed out from between her brows, and her lips were curved slightly upward, as though she'd seen something amusing.

"What?" he asked, letting his smile widen, ridiculously happy to see her look so lighthearted. "Do I have toast crumbs on my nose? Rundown sauce on my chin?"

She chuckled, shaking her head, and didn't answer his question, only saying, "I'd like to put up the decorations after we leave here. I think they'll make me get into the Christmas spirit a little more. I've missed feeling—what was the word you used—*festive*?"

And, suddenly, the day got brighter.

"Great," he said, grinning. "You'll love some of the ornaments I found. They're perfect."

CHAPTER TWELVE

Chloe hadn't been sure what to expect about Jamaica at Christmas but never in her wildest dreams had it included people in Santa hats and reindeer headbands dancing in the sea. Yet, she thought with a grin, forever after, if the words *Christmas* and *Jamaica* should ever be thrown together in her hearing, this was the scene she'd immediately recall.

Maiden Cay turned out to be nothing more than a sandbar out in the Caribbean Sea, about a twenty-minute boat ride from Morgan's Harbor Marina in Port Royal. It was, though, a popular spot for Kingstonians to party. With a bar and a sound system pumping out reggae, calypso, dancehall and, somewhat incongruously, Christmas music set up on the cay, it was well equipped for fun.

Vessels of various sizes were anchored in two crescent shapes on either side of the cay, many lashed together so people could pass from boat to boat when not in the water or onshore. Marlon Mattison's boat, being bigger than many of the others, had been anchored farther offshore in deeper water by itself.

It was quite a sight, and as Chloe stood waist deep in the water, she couldn't help thinking how lovely it all was. The sea was crystal clear, the sky bright blue with just a few fluffy clouds for emphasis. All around her, people laughed and shouted and sang, seemingly having the time of their lives.

"Hey, grab that for me, nuh?" someone shouted nearby, and Chloe turned in time to see a Santa hat floating near Marlon's boat. As she watched, too far away to help, Sam handed his dark glasses to someone, stepped up onto the gunwale and then executed a flawless shallow dive into the sea. With his broad shoulders and tapered torso, as well as truly masculine, muscular legs, he really did swimwear justice!

With a few easy strokes, he got to the hat. Plucking it from the water, he stuck the sopping thing on his head at a rakish angle and started swimming to hand it back to its owner.

Chloe turned away, not wanting to be caught staring, but there was no way to ignore her visceral reaction. Her skin prickled as though the temperature had suddenly risen, and a low throb started up in her belly, reminding her about the night before and the intensity of pleasure they'd shared.

She hadn't meant to sleep with him again, but somehow it had seemed completely natural after the laughter and teasing they'd shared decorating her flat.

She'd been enchanted as she opened boxes and bags and seen the ornaments he'd brought. While there were the requisite balls, stars and bells, he'd also brought a series of glass ornaments painted with island scenes.

"I thought you could keep those as mementoes," he'd said, as she exclaimed at their beauty. "One of my cousins paints them and I was fortunate enough to get a set before she sold out."

There were six balls in the series featuring Dunn's River Falls, a market scene, a beach view, Jonkanoo dancers, a raft being propelled down a bamboo-lined river, and finally, Devon House.

As she'd cupped that last one in her hands, she'd been overcome by a rush of tenderness for the man who'd gifted it to her. She'd turned away as she thanked him so he wouldn't be able to read any of what she was feeling in her eyes.

When it came to Sam, her emotions were all over the place, and she didn't know what to do about it.

Propelled by a need she couldn't seem to overcome, she glanced back toward the boat again, forcing herself to take in the entire scene, although her gaze wanted to seek out Sam, and only Sam.

Kendrick and his brother were standing near the cabin door, chatting with one of the other passengers, and as she watched, all three burst into laughter, making her smile.

Rashida was dancing, in no way hindered by her belly, which was at the stage where it seemed to get bigger each day. She seemed to have figured out how to use her stomach as a counterbalance for her shaking booty, and Chloe could only hope she'd be that chipper when she was seven months along.

For a moment the sun seemed to dim, as Dr. Hall's warnings regarding her chances of carrying the baby to term crossed Chloe's mind and had to be pushed away.

No. She was determined to keep a positive attitude. As Granny always said, "Never trouble trouble, till trouble trouble yuh!"

Finally, she let her eyes track toward where Sam was, still in the water at the side of the vessel, looking up and speaking to one of the women on board.

Jealousy fired through her, and Chloe made herself turn back toward the sandbar, although now she wasn't seeing anything but her own silliness.

What right did she have to care about whether Sam was talking to some tiny, cute, perfectly petite and gorgeous woman?

None.

His baby growing in her womb—and her sleeping with him the night before—gave her no hold over him whatsoever.

Now, if her hormones would just settle down and stop making her emotions swing wildly all over the place, she'd be fine.

The music had changed from soca to what seemed to be a very popular reggae tune, and a cheer went up on the cay. Because of the increase in the noise level, Chloe didn't realize Sam was approaching until suddenly he was beside her.

"Here," he said, holding out the wide-brimmed straw hat he'd insisted she buy the day before. "This will shield you a bit from the sun."

Dammit, now she was getting all gooey because he cared enough to be concerned about her getting burnt.

"Thank you," she said, taking the hat with a little smile but not looking at him. Sam, wet and slick from swimming was a far too potent turn-on. Best not to commit that image to memory. "I have on sunscreen, though."

"Yeah, but a hat is even better, although you still get the reflected glare off the water."

She murmured something incomprehensible in reply and set the hat on her head, glad that she'd pulled her hair back into a low, messy bun so it would fit.

"You having a good time?" Sam dipped down into the water so his head was lower than hers, as though wanting to be able to see her face. "I was worried that the weather wouldn't cooperate, but it's perfect for a beach session."

Chloe nodded. "I'm having a ball. The music is great, and the setting couldn't be more beautiful, although I'll admit it seems strange to see Santa hats and Christmas lights on boats in the middle of the ocean."

Sam laughingly agreed. "Everyone's excited for Christmas this year. Normally people wait until December to put up their decorations, but last year no one felt much of the spirit because of the pandemic, so I think they're trying to make up for it."

"I like it," Chloe replied. "The spirit of the season coming alive around me in a gloriously warm tropical setting."

"I'm glad," he replied, lifting a hand to wipe his face. "You don't mind me hanging out with you here, do you?"

She shook her head, knowing what he meant. Although she didn't know if he'd mentioned their relationship to Kendrick or anyone else, she still hadn't told Rashida or even Cora anything, even though she was tempted.

Was embarrassment holding her back?

She didn't think so. After all, they were all adults—both Sam and herself single—and she didn't think her friends would turn up their noses at her because of her actions.

No. If she were scrupulously honest with herself, there was a part of her that wanted to hug all of it—Sam, the baby, even just the fun afternoon of decorating—to herself for a while longer. Eventually there would have to be explanations and discussions, but for the moment, Chloe liked the sense of being isolated from all of that.

It also gave her more time to figure out what she was doing and to try to decipher Sam's actions in a rational manner.

Part of her wanted to believe Sam was going to be the present, nurturing father he seemed to be trying to convince her he could and would be. The other part, the cynical one that still stung from life with Finn, told her not to get her hopes up.

And then there was the part that melted a little more with each smile he sent her way. Each glance from those twinkling, mischievous eyes. Each touch, accidental or on purpose, they exchanged. Every caress they shared.

That part—which seemed to grow increasingly strong—weakened her resolve to distance herself from him. Instead, it rejoiced each time he invited her somewhere or just called to find out how she was. Not to mention how it exulted at being in his arms and the sense of freedom she found in his lovemaking.

All those bits of her were frankly at war, and she admitted the inconsistency of her thought patterns was annoying. Was that contrariness leading her to make unfortunate choices? She really didn't know what she wanted, so even following her heart wasn't left as a viable option.

"Hey, Sam. Chloe. You want something to eat?"

They both looked back toward the boat, and then Sam lifted an eyebrow at her, making her heart do a silly little stutter.

"Are you hungry?"

Needing to make things light, to break out from the weight of all she was experiencing, she cocked one eyebrow right back at him.

"You want to feed me again, don't you?"

He laughed, but there was a gleam in his eyes that said there were other things he'd rather do just then.

"Always. I can't have you withering away on my watch."

It was her turn to laugh then. "I don't think I'm in any danger of that. I've already put on a couple of pounds since I've been here."

His eyelids drooped, and the look he gave her was incendiary. "You're perfect."

For a long moment, she couldn't breathe, her breath hitching somewhere beneath her diaphragm, her pulse going haywire.

How could he do that to her with just a look and two simple words?

"Come on," she said, the words a little choked. "I should have a little something."

And she struck out for the boat, not waiting to see if he was following.

Once on board, she toweled off and got her food. Purposefully making her way to where Rashida was sitting, she took the last spot on the bench and tucked in, not joining the conversation. Instead, she swung her foot in time to the song now playing, as though caught up in the music. Pretending to listen to what happened when Santa got stuck in a mango tree was better than trying to figure out her complicated life.

Sam really, really wanted to punch Marlon in the mouth, even though they'd known each other since they were in nappies, and he was, through Kendrick, an honorary part of the family.

"Ooh, bwoy. Mi can't tek it. That woman is making me sweat." He turned to his brother, a scowl on his face. "Explain again why it is she's been here almost a month, an' mi jus' a-meet her?"

His rhapsodies over Chloe had been almost nonstop since the start of the trip. If Kendrick didn't put a stop to it soon, Sam might find himself facing charges of mutiny.

It was very bad form to toss a captain off his own vessel.

He'd finally been unable to keep it to himself anymore and told Kendrick he was seeing Chloe, although out of respect for her, he'd made it sound casual and hadn't mentioned the baby. It had been hard not to say something to his best friend about that, because Sam teetered constantly between insane joy and gut-wrenching fear every time he thought about the pregnancy. Being able to share those emotions with his level-headed friend would surely have gone a long way toward calming him down. But Chloe was adamant about not telling anyone, and Sam knew he couldn't abuse her trust that way.

Now Marlon's drooling was just aggravating him beyond bearing. Rather than let his temper get the better of him, Sam stuffed the last forkful of food into his mouth and tried to tune the other two men out, but it wasn't easy.

The truth was, although he'd tried to hide it from Chloe, he was still annoyed from the night before, and Marlon with his nonsense wasn't improving his mood.

He'd thought he and Chloe had had a good time. No, a great time. She'd seemed so happy and relaxed as they put up the tree and decorated it. And afterward, when he couldn't keep his hands off her a moment more, she hadn't resisted even for a second. In fact, she'd taken their first kiss from sweet to carnal in the blink of an eye.

Then, just when he'd thought everything was perfect, she'd kicked him out and refused to come home with him, to boot.

"You could bring your clothes for tomorrow," he said, while she sat up in bed watching him. He was trying to dress as slowly as possible, hoping she'd change her mind and tell him to come back. "Then we can drive out to the marina together."

"Kendrick and Rashida have already said they'll come and collect me," she'd replied, as unmovable as Blue Mountain Peak itself. "So it's all arranged."

He couldn't help realizing she didn't want him hanging about—and didn't want Rashida or Kendrick knowing they were seeing each other.

Ridiculous to feel used and, frankly, outmaneuvered.

Here he was, trying his best to get their relationship normalized—if that were even possible—and she was ducking it at every turn.

"Woo-ee, look at dat. Look at dat."

Sam had been trying his best not to look at Chloe, but at Marlon's words, his gaze swung right to her, only to see Rashida teaching her one of the new dance steps. Chloe was laughing, her face alight with mirth, while her body…

Oh, Lawd. The swivel of her hips, the way her

breasts moved beneath the thin material of her swimsuit made his brain short-circuit and his body grow hard between one breath and the next.

Was he even actually breathing?

From the tightness of his chest, he thought perhaps not but couldn't somehow seem to care.

She moved that way when they were in bed together, with unfettered joy and the kind of innate sensuality that no red-blooded man could ignore.

Sam wanted to go over there, swing her into his arms and dance with her. Or cover her up with a towel and hide her from all the other appreciative gazes now affixed to her luscious body.

Marlon headed that way and Sam watched with building anger as the other man tried to pry Chloe away from Rashida so as to dance with her himself.

"You know, if you murder Marlon, you'll not only go to jail but Mummy will never talk to you again. And she's your biggest fan."

"I won't murder him," Sam replied to Kendrick, while keeping his eyes on the ongoing drama at the stern of the boat. "But I might do him a damage."

Kendrick snorted. "Yeah, but it's your own fault, man. You've hardly said a word to Chloe all day, besides that one little dip together. No wonder Marlon thinks she's a free agent."

Sam tried to shrug but ended up with his shoulders stuck up by his ears for a moment as Marlon put his arm around Chloe's waist and they started moving from side to side in sync.

"That's the way she seems to want it. I asked her to move in with me—just for the rest of the time she's here—and she turned me down."

"Hmm." Kendrick took a swig of Red Stripe from his bottle, as though giving himself time to figure out what to say next. "Rashida told me Chloe's been through a tough couple of years. Maybe she doesn't want any more complications in her life right now. And knowing our families, her living with you, even for a little while, would definitely bring complications. I'd go so far as to say high drama."

He'd pointed out to Chloe that, whether she liked it or not, the baby would definitely cause both complications and drama, so they might as well get out ahead of it. She'd remained unmoved.

Kendrick gave him a long, solemn look before saying, "I've never seen you like this before. You sure this is just one of your usual flings?"

It was on the tip of his tongue to blurt it all out, but he pulled back at the last moment.

"Yeah, what else could it be when we live an ocean apart?"

"Huh." Kendrick took another swig from his bottle and shook his head. "You tell me."

"Nothing more," he said, shortly. But he'd had enough of watching Marlon pawing Chloe and whispering in her ear. "Excuse me."

Stopping at the cooler, Sam grabbed a bottle of water and went over to where Chloe was now sitting on one of the benches, Marlon looming over her like a John Crow.

Plopping down beside her, he forced a smile and held out the water. "Best to keep hydrated in this heat."

"Go weh, Sam." Marlon sounded genuinely put out, as though he had a chance with Chloe, and Sam was blocking it. "Yuh nuh see me talking to the beautiful lady?"

It would be so easy, so shockingly easy, to just say *Back off, Marlon, she's mine. And she's going to be my baby mother, so you can't have her.*

Sam bit back the words, but they were on the tip of his tongue.

Instead, he just smiled, baring his teeth quite a bit more than was absolutely necessary, and said, "Isn't that Toni over there, looking for you? She was asking about you earlier."

"Lawd," said Marlon, looking around like the guilty man he was, trying to spot his ex-lover. "Hide mi!"

As he hurried off toward the boat's cabin, Chloe turned a laughing face Sam's way and said, "That was pretty mean."

Now he could shrug, unfettered and unrepentant.
"All's fair in love and war. And that was war."

Chloe's laughter shouldn't make him so happy,
but it did.

And it was at that exact moment, Sam knew
he was in deep, deep trouble.

CHAPTER THIRTEEN

THE DAY AFTER the Maiden Cay excursion, Chloe woke up reaching for Sam in the bed beside her, although she didn't know why. Since the first time they'd been together at his place and fallen asleep, she'd been careful not to spend the night with him. There was something so incredibly intimate about spending the night in the same bed and waking up with him, that she'd been determined not to do it.

It felt like a step too far.

But nevertheless, here she was, her arm outflung, palm down on the cool sheet beside her, feeling lonely.

"Contrarian," she chided herself, rubbing her hand back and forth. "This is what you wanted, isn't it?"

Yet although she'd enjoyed the trip the day before, it had shown that perhaps this *wasn't* really what she wanted.

Sam had made it obvious on Saturday that he wanted her to come home with him and then travel together to the marina the next morning. When she'd refused and gone with Kendrick and Rashida, he'd obviously taken it as meaning she didn't want anyone to know they knew each other and had acted accordingly. Besides the brief moments in the sea, bringing her water a couple of times and rescuing her from Kendrick's brother, he'd paid her little mind. And even after Marlon had scurried away, Sam had quickly excused himself, and that had been the last time they spoke.

She'd half hoped, half expected that he'd offer to drive her home, but once they got back to the dock, she'd seen him have a quick word with Kendrick, and then he'd left. And he hadn't called to make sure she'd got home okay either.

Now, as she got up, she wondered if he'd call as he usually did, to ask how she was doing.

If the boat trip, and that desolate feeling she'd woken up with this morning told her anything, it was that she didn't want to go on the way they were. Sneaking about, pretending there was nothing going on between them.

Spending nights in separate beds.

Moving to this next step was frankly terrifying, but at this point, she had to admit certain truths, if only to herself.

Sam was right when he'd said that if people knew they'd been seeing each other in Jamaica, it would make the eventual baby revelation easier.

Also, although she was leery of getting in too deep with him, there was something between them that couldn't be denied. A scorching passion unlike anything she'd known before that made her feel better about herself, just in its expression. After her divorce she'd wanted to grow, to become stronger, less namby-pamby, and although she certainly didn't know why, being with Sam seemed a step in the right direction.

Lastly—and it had taken her a while to even realize it—once she was back in England and the baby was born, an opportunity like this would never come again. She was determined to devote herself to raising her child and being the best mother she could be. There would be no time for love affairs and grand passions. If she didn't take advantage of this chance to enjoy Sam, and the woman she was with him, it would be lost forever.

She was taking Dr. Owens's clinic that evening, so wasn't scheduled to start work until later in the morning, and was inclined to curse about the extra time it gave her to think. On a morning like this, there would be nothing better than activity to keep her mind occupied, but instead, she was stuck in the flat, one ear cocked, in the hopes Sam would call.

Although what, exactly, she planned to say to him, she didn't know.

And when the phone finally did ring, it wasn't him at all, but Rashida.

"Chloe!" Rashida's voice was at full volume, and Chloe pulled the phone away from her ear while stifling a laugh. "Girl, can you believe it's Monday already? Where did the damn weekend go?"

"There was a weekend?" she teased. "No one told me that."

Her friend laughed. "Remember those two days when you didn't go to the hospital? That's what that was."

"Ah, thank you for the update."

"You're too funny. But listen, I want to make up for missing our shopping trip. Let's get together this evening, and we can go to a few stores. They're starting to stay open a bit later and I still need to do my Christmas shopping."

"Actually, I can't make it this evening since I have clinic from six to nine. But I do need your help, and I'm hoping we can do that shopping trip later in the week? I need a dress."

"Ooh, what for?"

Here was a prime opportunity to get her relationship with Sam out in the open, although she'd enjoyed the intrigue and secrecy of it for a while. If Rashida found out through gossip or from Kendrick, she'd probably be upset and it could cost Chloe a friendship she'd come to value.

"For Sam's mother's gala, next Saturday."

There was a long, pregnant pause, and then Rashida asked, "Sam Powell's mother?"

She said it as though she'd never heard his name before and Chloe sat down, settling in for the interrogation. "Yes."

"I didn't know you knew Sam well enough to be invited to the fundraiser. And if yesterday was anything to go by, I'd still say it wasn't possible you did. How on earth did that come about?"

"Well, Sam and I had met before, at a medical conference, and he's been checking on me since I got here. Well, more than checking on me, really. We've been sort of seeing each other."

"Hold on," Rashida said, her voice rising a little. "You knew each other from before? And you've been *seeing* each other, recently? How come Kendrick never gave me that piece of suss?"

"Maybe he didn't know?"

With a kiss of her teeth, Rashida let her opinion of that statement be understood.

"Those two are thick as thieves. Have been since they were little boys. He knows, and didn't tell me. Hold on. You never told me either!"

Chloe chuckled, even though it really was no laughing matter. "It never came up. Besides, Sam and I are just casual friends."

"Huh…" Chloe could almost hear the gears grinding in Rashida's head. "Well, my advice, my friend, is that you keep it casual. Sam's a great guy but not the settling-down type."

Chloe forced a laugh. "Who said anything about settling down? That's a huge leap, from casual friends to happy-ever-after, isn't it?"

"Just saying," came the swift reply. "He's not a dog—doesn't lead women on—but there's more than one woman who found out the hard way that he meant it when he said he wasn't interested in anything more than a good time. There were a couple who felt that because they'd slept with him and hung out together for a few months, it was going to last forever."

"I harbor no such delusions," Chloe assured her friend, keeping her tone light even though she felt as if a rock had settled in her chest. "Sam's just being kind, and we're just having a bit of fun together. After all, I'm only here for another four weeks or so."

"Long enough to fall in love," Rashida said, her voice positively dripping with warning. "Please, just remember what I've said."

"Don't worry." Making the words casual and breezy was difficult, but Chloe thought she managed it. "I just finished with a horrid divorce, remember? Getting serious about any man is the last thing in my plan, believe me."

And she realized she actually meant it. She'd given her all to Finn, only to have it thrown back in her face. There was no way she'd be willing to risk that again. From now on, if she was giving her all, it would be to her child.

Her little miracle.

And though she was willing to share the baby with Sam, her own heart and life would be off-limits once she left Jamaica.

"All right, my friend." Rashida still didn't sound totally convinced but seemed disinclined to belabor her point. "Just don't get hurt—or hurt Sam." She tacked the last on as though it was an afterthought. "Mind you, it would be great if you both *did* fall in love, and I get to keep you here in Jamaica."

"How do you know I wouldn't convince him to move to England instead?" Chloe teased, and she laughed when Rashida replied with a long, juicy kissing of her teeth.

"Then I'd have to hunt you down and do you damage," she said. "Kendrick would be like a headless chicken without Sam around, and our phone bills would be through the roof. Are you free tomorrow? I know just the place to take you to get an outfit."

After making plans for the following evening, they said their goodbyes and rang off.

It was strange, she thought to herself as she made another cup of tea, but the conversation with Rashida had somehow steadied her mind. Now, even more so than before, she knew for a fact that the only person whose emotions she needed to protect were her own.

According to Rashida, Sam Powell wasn't

the type to get attached, and Chloe valued her friend's insight. Rashida had known Sam a great deal longer than Chloe had and could be relied on to provide an honest opinion.

So, Chloe should be able to enjoy their renewed physical relationship and let it be known they were seeing each other without fear—fear for him, at any rate.

But, of course, her foremost thoughts must be for the future of their child, and no amount of pleasure could be allowed to jeopardize it—or the relationship with its father.

Even if Sam wasn't willing to consider that, Chloe had to.

Sam yawned, more annoyed than usual at the slow pace of the traffic on his way to work. Despite the sun and sea air, which usually had a soporific effect on him, he hadn't slept well.

This whole situation with Chloe had him messed up—bad-bad.

Tossing and turning, alternately angry at the way she'd acted as though she hardly knew him and frustrated because he wanted her in his bed, he'd spent a restless night.

He'd turned Kendrick's words over in his head, wondering if Chloe really was avoiding whatever drama publicly being with him would cause.

Millie Hall had said she should avoid unnecessary stress, too, although she'd conceded that modern life was often inherently stressful, especially when one was a physician.

Perhaps for Chloe's sake, he should back off. Give her enough room to breathe, without him trying to press her into a situation she didn't want?

Everything inside him rebelled at the thought. He wasn't trying to push her to do anything untoward, was he? All he wanted was to make sure she understood he was committed—to supporting her and the baby, at any rate.

But he hadn't ruled out marrying her to keep her and his child in Jamaica or at least have a solid footing on which to move to the UK.

Migration was an idea he never thought he'd ever consider, and realizing it had been percolating in the back of his mind was something of a revelation.

He honestly loved his life. He loved his country, his friends and his family, no matter how annoying they could be at times. Yet here he was, considering giving it all up to be with a woman who clearly wasn't even willing to let people know they were a couple.

That made him snort.

They weren't a couple. At least, not in Chloe's eyes. His reaction to seeing Marlon and a couple of the other men out at Maiden Cay try to chat her up told him he saw the situation much differently, but his opinion didn't seem to matter right now.

It should make him angry, but instead he just felt baffled and a little sad.

So he'd decided to give Chloe some more space. If she wanted to talk, she knew where to find him, but right now, he didn't feel he was in the best frame of mind to seek her out, even with a call.

As the traffic started moving, finally, and he had to navigate around a truck that had broken down, his phone rang, and he answered without checking the caller ID.

"Dr. Sam Powell."

"Sam, you dutty dwag. How you nevah tell mi seh you and Chloe was an item?"

At Rashida's words his heart stopped for a second and then settled back down. Scowling, he replied, "Kendrick told you?"

"No! And you wait till I see him later. I goin' give him a tongue-lashing like you wouldn't believe. I was just talking to Chloe, and she spilled the beans. She said you invited her to Miss Norma's gala, and that the two of you are carrying straw."

Now his heart was galloping, but he'd known Rashida too long to be taken in by her overexuberant style of speaking. Sometimes she played fool to catch wise, saying something she knew wasn't strictly true as a way to get a person to say more than they should.

"Carrying straw?"

Using that particular expression usually carried a connotation of a serious relationship rather than casual.

"Well, okay, she didn't make it sound as though it was that serious. But she said you were seeing each other, and I man vex that I'm apparently the last to know."

Sam couldn't help chuckling. "Rashida, you're only the second person to know, not counting Chloe and me, so you're way ahead of everyone else."

"Huh." She didn't sound appeased. "So, you're introducing her to your fam on Saturday, eh? What are you going to tell them?"

"Nothing, other than her name."

"Sam!"

"What? Is there something else I should tell them?"

Had Chloe told Rashida about the baby too? If so, he was sure it would be all over Kingston—and probably much farther afield—before the day was out.

"I don't know. Is there?"

"No," he said firmly, realizing she was fishing again. "Don't make it out to be more than it is."

Rashida kissed her teeth.

"You know what, Sam Powell? I'm glad Chloe has such a good head on her shoulders and doesn't seem to be taking you too seriously. She's been through a lot, and I just wanted to tell you that if you hurt her—"

"Okay. I get the drift," he said, breaking into her tirade. The last thing he needed was to be reminded of just how tenuous his situation was and how easy it would be to mess up. "Have a good day, and go easy on Kendrick. He didn't say anything because I asked him not to."

"*Harrumph.* Now you're really on sinking sands, my friend, making a man keep secrets from his wife."

Sam only laughed and said goodbye.

As soon as Rashida hung up, Sam texted Kendrick on his work phone, making sure his friend knew that his wife was on the warpath.

And as he finally made it almost to the hospital and the traffic started to flow freely, he realized he was whistling.

Chloe had broken the seal of secrecy she'd put on their relationship, and now Sam felt free to act.

Act how, exactly, he wasn't sure, but he'd figure it out.

CHAPTER FOURTEEN

CHLOE PUT HER mind firmly on work, although her brain wanted, very badly, to wander its way to thinking about Sam. He hadn't called that morning, and she wasn't sure whether to be annoyed, sad or happy.

More of her previously unknown contrariness coming to the fore, causing her all kinds of mental issues.

The first part of the day dragged, with only the news that Kadisha Barnes was responding well to treatment for hyperthyroidism to brighten Chloe's spirits. Then, just before the start of the evening clinic, she found herself tempted to call or text Sam but talked herself out of it.

Realistically, although she felt more sanguine about their relationship and the ramifications of being seen to be involved with him, knowledge of the inherent risk refused to be banished.

There was no escaping habit, and that darned conservative streak so carefully implanted in her by her previous experiences refused to lie down and shut up.

Of course, if things went poorly between them, she could simply walk away. Return home, and leave him to sort out how he was going to react to fatherhood and whether he'd be available for their child or not.

Yet that didn't sit quite right with her. Indeed, she didn't see in Sam the type of man who would distance himself from his child just to spite or avoid its mother. If anything, he'd be even more intent on making sure he did all he could for his offspring, in as honorable a way as was possible.

He had definite strength of character, and his reactions to news of her pregnancy had given her the idea that he was all in when it came to being a dad.

Talking to Rashida had taken away some of her worries, but Chloe was, by nature, the kind of person who picked and picked at problems until she understood them. Acting without complete understanding—or at least understanding all she could—didn't come easy to her at all.

"But sometimes you have to take a leap of faith," she muttered to herself, while shrugging into her lab coat. "Be brave. At least I'm pretty sure *he* won't be hurt by whatever happens."

And, she also knew her own strength. The breakdown of her marriage, and the realization of how little she'd gained for all the time spent trying to nurture and uphold it, were painful but valuable lessons.

As long as she had her baby, she would survive, and they both would thrive, with or without Sam.

That gave her some peace, and she was smiling as she went in to greet her first patient.

By nine thirty, she had seen the last person on the list and was finishing up her charts when the nurse popped her head around the door to say good-night.

"Thank you so much for keeping everything flowing tonight, Doreen. I appreciate all your help."

Nurse Doreen grinned. "You're welcome, Dr. Bailey. And I have to say, your understanding of patois is coming along nicely."

Chloe laughed with her and thanked her again with a wave. Doreen had been nurse on duty during the Alice in Wonderland diagnosis, and had had to act as interpreter between the boy's mother and Chloe. Although she'd grown up hearing her grandparents speaking patois at home, there were some times when comprehension failed her, badly. And that could be fatal when one was a doctor.

Locking up behind her, she made her way out to the parking lot and looked around for her driver Delroy's car, but it was nowhere to be seen. Instead, there was Sam, leaning on the front of his 4X4, arms crossed, sexier than should be allowed.

He walked to meet her halfway across the parking lot, and Chloe tried to will her heart to slow down but to no avail.

"I told Delroy I was here to take you home," he said. "I hope you don't mind?"

"Not at all."

And suddenly, seeing him again like this, something inside her settled and grew quiet.

They were in his vehicle, heading for her flat when he said, "You told Rashida about us."

"Yes, but not about the baby. I didn't think that was necessary."

He was silent for a moment and then asked, "Does this mean your objections to having people know we're seeing each other no longer apply?"

"I still have some reservations," she replied, trying to be as honest as she could. "But I realize you were right when you said it would make things easier in the long run."

Sam exhaled, and the corner of his lips twitched upward momentarily before settling back into a line.

"I'm glad."

He said it simply. A statement of fact. Yet her pulse started racing, like a crazy thing.

"Why?"

"Because I'm tired of pretending we're just friends."

How to interpret that? Chloe decided not to read too much into it. Rashida had cautioned her, and she was taking her warning about Sam's aversion to serious relationships to heart. She didn't doubt it had taken some determination on his part to not already be married. Any woman with a grain of sense would have snapped him up in a heartbeat.

"Well, you don't need to anymore."

They drove the rest of the way in silence, but it wasn't uncomfortable. It felt...peaceful. As though both of them had reached a place of, if not clarity, then something close to that.

He came upstairs with her, and she wasn't sure whether he would come in or not. But there was something she realized she wanted and was willing to take the chance of having.

So when she opened the door, she turned to him and said, "If you give me a few minutes, I'll pack a bag."

He froze, his gaze searching hers, but she held it as understanding dawned in his eyes.

"We'll have to move the decorations to my house," he said, his eyes gleaming, and a little smile playing across his lips.

"Sure," she said, giving a little shrug. "We can do that when I come to get the rest of my stuff during the week."

His answering grin told her that even if she

wasn't doing the right thing, it was what they both wanted.

And that was enough for her, in the moment.

They were back in his car and heading for his home when it struck Sam that there was something very different about Chloe this evening, but it took a while for Sam to put his finger on what it was.

She was more relaxed than he'd seen her since her arrival on the island—chatting casually with him about the clinic that evening and her upcoming newspaper interview that Thursday. The entire time, her voice was serene, occasionally amused but without the edge it so often had.

This was a Chloe he didn't know. The first night they'd met, the conversation was casual—determinedly so—and flirtatious. They'd both kept it light, even when the sexual tension between them became obvious. Since she'd turned up in Jamaica, their interactions had been stressful, unpredictable, and there was no wonder. Just seeing each other again had been a shock. The baby revelation had stunned them. Almost every encounter had been fraught with questions and decisions needing to be made.

Suddenly it felt as though she'd put all of it aside, and he wasn't sure what to make of or how to handle it.

With an internal shrug, Sam decided to just go

with the flow. After all, what other choice did he have just now?

He also knew he had a tendency to bulldoze his way through situations, but as he'd told her honestly, he had also been used to only really having to think about himself. Only with his family and closest friends was he willing to compromise and make allowances.

She was part of his family, whether she liked it or not, so he was willing to put his own wishes aside to make her happy.

Not that he had anything to complain about right now. She was in his SUV, and they were on their way to his house, where she would spend the night in his bed. By inference, she'd decided to give in to his request to stay with him for the rest of her trip, which was what he'd wanted.

Was it really giving in, though? Or did Chloe have reasons of her own for the decision?

Did it matter?

Sam considered and decided it did.

Until they started communicating properly, there was way too much margin for error. As a surgeon, he was used to calculating risk over benefit and knew it could mean the difference between life and death. A satisfactory outcome or one that did nobody any good.

"Why did you decide to come and stay with me?"

From the corner of his eye, he saw her head

turn as though she was surprised by the question, and she seemed to consider the question for an awfully long time before she answered.

"When I spoke to Rashida, she warned me not to take you too seriously—that you're not the kind to want a long-term relationship. In a funny way, that was reassuring. It let me know that you weren't in danger of getting in over your head."

He didn't know whether to be hurt by his friend's assessment of his character, even if it was true, but pushed the thought aside for the moment.

"What about you, Chloe? You're not worried about yourself?"

"Getting attached?" Her little huff of laughter was, for some unknown reason, painful. "Sam, I'm a realist. I have to be, with a baby to think about. I'll only be here for another month, and once I go back, it'll be to put plans in motion for myself and my child. I'm not stupid enough to jeopardize it all by falling for you. And even if I did, I'd deal with it."

"That sounds almost cynical."

He wanted to keep her talking, learn how her mind worked, gain some insight into her heart and her soul. It shouldn't be important for him to do, but somehow it was.

"I've already been through the fire. I'm tempered. Hardened, to a degree." She laid her head back against the seat, and when he glanced her way, she was smiling, just slightly. "I'm also aware that this is probably the last time I'll get to do something even slightly crazy, like moving into the house of a man I really hardly know. So, with that being the case, I'm parking my risk aversion and I'm simply going to enjoy myself. If that's okay with you?"

"It is," he said, matching her matter-of-fact calm, even when inside, he wasn't quite as sure as he sounded.

And as he led her up to his bed a little while later, he knew it was more than okay with him.

In fact, having her there was almost perfect.

Frighteningly so, when he took her attitude toward him into consideration.

CHAPTER FIFTEEN

HAVING MADE THE decision to stay with Sam, Chloe refused to second-guess it and, by the end of that first week, realized she was happier than she could remember being for a long time.

Living with Sam was surprisingly easy. Used to Finn's constant demands and complaints, she'd been braced for something similar, but her fears in that regard never materialized. Instead, Sam was considerate and almost ridiculously courteous. Once she stopped waiting for the other shoe to drop and reminded herself she was there for only a short time, Chloe began to really relax.

Kendrick had been surprisingly urbane about the change in her address and assured her he'd reassign Delroy, who was on staff at the hospital, so he wouldn't be losing his job because she didn't need him anymore. Besides that, he made no comment to her, either positive or negative.

Rashida, on the other hand, seemed to be beside herself.

"I've never known Sam to have a woman live

with him," she said, on the evening she took Chloe to buy a frock for the charity do. "You sure you two aren't planning something permanent?"

"I'm only here until January first, then I'm gone. This is as permanent as it is going to get."

Rashida had slid her such a look of disbelief Chloe couldn't help laughing.

"Honestly, we're just having a bit of fun. Don't read anything more into it or you'll hurt your brain."

That had made Rashida chuckle, although she still didn't look totally convinced.

Everywhere, there were the signs of Christmas now. Lights twinkled, decorations gleamed and white euphorbias set off the bright reds and gentle pinks of poinsettias. There was a sense of excitement in the air, and the oft-time languid movements of the city folk seemed to speed up until there was an extra bounce in their steps.

For the first time in years, Chloe felt a part of it all rather than the season being a chore of shopping and taking care of everyone else's needs and wishes. When Sam helped her pack up the decorations they'd put up in her flat not too long before, she had a little pang of melancholy, as though it was a harbinger of endings. That faded quickly, though, when he insisted on their doing the entire process all over again, only at his home instead. By the time they had finished, the living room had a jolly, festive air, and Chloe's cheeks ached from laughing at Sam's antics. He, by the simple method of being himself and showing honest enjoyment of their time together, had once more totally transformed her mood.

That Thursday, she had the dreaded newspaper interview, which turned out to be far less stressful than she'd envisioned. The reporter had been overjoyed to find out that Chloe's grandparents had been born on the island since, as she said with a laugh, "We Jamaicans are quite sure the island is the source of all things great."

Then she had her next appointment with Dr. Hall, who started with a physical examination along with lots of questions about how Chloe had been feeling.

"It's been surprisingly smooth," Chloe told her, as the doctor measured her abdomen. "I have crackers beside my bed, just in case, but I haven't had any morning sickness, and my breasts are a little tender but nothing unbearable."

"Still tired?" Dr. Hall put away her measuring tape and began to prepare the machine for the ultrasound. Chloe's heart rate picked up, and Sam shifted position so he could see the monitor better.

"A bit. Those unscheduled naps—the ones that sneak up on me—have abated, though."

"It should get better from now on." She had the ultrasound wand in her hand and sent Chloe a slight smile. "Ready to see the baby?"

"Yes, please," she said, hardly able to breathe.

"I'm guessing it's no use asking you two whether you want to know the sex or not," she said, as she squirted gel onto Chloe's stomach. "You'll figure it out for yourselves, if not this time, then the next."

Neither she nor Sam answered, and when Chloe sent him a fleeting glance, she found his eyes were trained on the monitor, his face intent and somehow stern.

Then the wand was sliding across her skin, and Chloe's gaze flew to the screen.

It took what felt like forever for Dr. Hall to get her bearings, although it wasn't more than a few seconds. And then...

"There."

It took a moment for the swishing sound to register as the heartbeat, because Chloe was mesmerized by the image. Her medical side traced the form, searched, saw nothing but pure perfection in the tiny being nestled inside her belly.

"Oh," she gasped, and felt Sam's fingers squeeze hers. She hadn't even realized he'd taken her hand, until that moment.

"Looks like a girl," Dr. Hall said. "Although it's too early to be absolutely sure."

"A girl," Sam echoed, and there was no mistaking the wonder in his voice.

When she looked at him, he was still staring

at the ultrasound monitor, and Chloe could see his eyes were misty.

"Don't you start, Sam," she said, trying for a light tone, even though her throat was tight. "You know it doesn't take much to get me going nowadays."

Millie Hall glanced first at Sam and then Chloe and smiled.

"Yes, Sam, stop your nonsense before you make Mum cry too."

He laughed, but it sounded rusty. "You two leave me alone." And Chloe's heart gave a flip when he lifted her hand to his lips and kissed the back before saying, "If I want to get sappy over the first look at my baby, it's none of your business."

They all chuckled, but the tenderness of the moment stuck with Chloe, through Millicent Hall's recap of the appointment and the declaration that she was satisfied with the progress of the pregnancy. Even her admonishment to make sure they called her at the slightest discomfort didn't dim the glow surrounding Chloe's life as they left with a sonogram picture of their child.

That night when they made love, it was with a slow, gentle rhythm, as though the evening's events had lulled them into a new phase of their relationship. One that Chloe didn't allow herself to dwell on too much.

None of it changed the inevitable outcome, and

she refused to allow future sorrows, fears or uncertainty to cloud the beauty of the present.

Of course, there was still Sam's family to meet, but she just kept reminding herself that she wouldn't be around long enough for their opinion of her to really matter. And whatever trepidation she still felt on the Saturday evening of the gala event melted away under Sam's appreciative gaze when she came down the stairs.

"You look amazing," he said, taking her hand and twirling her slowly around.

Laughing, she replied, "Thank Rashida. She took me to the place she says she shops at almost exclusively when she isn't—in her words— 'grossly preggers.'"

And, even without his approval, she knew she was looking her best. The bright yellow silk of the dress made her skin glow, while the fitted bodice and flowing skirt set off her figure to perfection. She'd hesitated over her heels, knowing they weren't the best thing to be wearing, but she compromised by buying a slightly lower pair, telling Rashida she didn't have any with her that would match her gown.

Sam looked magnificent in his tuxedo, and she told him so, having the pleasure of seeing him look almost abashed at her words.

That was something else she'd discovered about him. For all his good looks, intelligence and strong will, he seemed almost unaware of his appeal. It was both surprising and endearing.

When they pulled up to the hotel where the ball was being held, Chloe took a deep breath.

"It'll be fine," Sam assured her, as the valet opened her door. "Just enjoy yourself, and don't worry about anyone."

The ballroom was stunning. Instead of what Chloe thought of as traditional Christmas decor, it was festooned with long streams of white orchids, tied with red velvet ribbons and set among evergreen boughs. That was something of a theme of the Jamaican Christmas, she realized. Because the white euphorbia and red poinsettias bloomed at that time of the year, red and white had become synonymous with the season.

It was crowded as people mingled during the cocktail hour, chatting and laughing. Chloe was a little staggered at the attendees' elegance, although she'd already noticed how beautifully Jamaican women dressed, no matter their occupation or social bracket.

"Come and meet the parents, and get it over with," Sam said, in an obviously teasing tone, putting his hand on her lower back to guide her toward the other side of the room. Partway across, he dipped his head to whisper into her ear, "Do you know how difficult it was for me to leave the house this evening? I just want to take you back home and slowly work that dress off you, running the silk over your skin to figure out which is softer."

Heat rushed down her spine, making her shiver, and she paused long enough to reply, just as softly, "I think, for comparison's sake, it would be better if I rub the silk *and* my skin over you, so you can properly decide."

The look he gave her was incendiary and full of promise.

"Deal," he replied, just as someone called his name, and he turned toward the sound.

"Sam, you finally made it." A woman, almost as tall as Sam, was on them and reached up to kiss his cheeks. She turned an interrogative expression Chloe's way and then, after a brief moment, smiled widely, "Oh, it's Dr. Bailey. How nice to see you again. I'm so glad you came."

"You've already met my sister, Mel?" Sam asked, his eyebrows high with surprise.

"Yes," Chloe replied, wondering how it was she hadn't noticed the family resemblance before.

"Dr. Bailey was at the clinic when I took Ali in for her last checkup, and I think what she said really got through to her. Her behavior has calmed down so much since then. Sam, I'll tell you all about it after this craziness is over. I don't know how Mummy keeps talking us into doing this year after year."

And then she was gone in a swirl of perfume

and velvet, making a beeline for a person at the side of the room who was beckoning to her.

"I feel a little silly, having not realized Mrs. Gabaldon was your sister," Chloe said, still stunned. "The two of you look very much alike."

Sam wrinkled his nose. "She isn't as handsome. Or so I've heard. Come on. Mummy and Daddy are holding court just over there."

His parents turned out to be nothing like what she'd expected. Mr. Powell was a head shorter than Sam, although very like him in physique, while Mrs. Powell had "stamped" the children with her unmistakably beautiful features. The couple was comfortably ensconced at the far end of the room, husband on his feet chatting with a group of people, wife seated in a comfortable chair, her walker close to hand.

And although Chloe found herself very much the object of close scrutiny by both, they were nothing but charming and friendly, leaving her to wonder if they knew about their son's current living arrangement.

When she asked Sam, while they were heading to the bar, he shrugged.

"Kingston may be a city, but in many ways, it's just a small town. If Rashida mentioned it to her mother, then mine no doubt will know."

Dinnertime found her and Sam at a table with Rashida, Kendrick and another couple, who were introduced to Chloe as longtime friends.

"Milton went to high school with us," Kendrick said. "And has never wavered in his devotion to the purple-and-white."

She took that as a reference to the school colors and was proved right when the men launched into a spirited debate about various sporting events that went right over her head.

"These damn men, with their Manning Cup and Champs," Milton's wife, Jacinth, grumbled, sending them a hard look. "In their thirties and still arguing about schoolboy sports. You'd think they'd have outgrown the fascination by now."

"What are men but overgrown boys anyway?" quipped Rashida, before taking a sip of her water. "Might as well let them go at it. It's harmless, one way or another."

And their talk turned to another topic of seemingly endless appeal to the Jamaicans Chloe had so far met—food. Specifically, Christmas fare.

"You should see my gungo peas tree." Jacinth all but crowed. "Laden. Positively laden with pods. And the sorrel is already picked and drying."

"Our sorrel is steeping," Rashida interjected. "It bore early this year, and I didn't want to wait. Oh, and I got some Jerusalem peas from the country."

They kindly explained, for Chloe's sake, that gungo peas, otherwise known as pigeon peas, used to be available exclusively at Christmas time, so were synonymous with the season. Jerusalem peas, she gathered, were like tiny red kidney beans and were hard to find because they weren't considered a cash crop.

"And you know all about sorrel, don't you?" Jacinth asked.

"Yes," Chloe laughed, familiar with the ruby-red drink, steeped with ginger and allspice and often "sweetened" with overproof rum, ubiquitous during the holiday season among Jamaicans. "Through my grandparents. You can buy the dried petals in the Jamaican stores back home, but British people always get confused by the name. To them, that's not something you use to make a drink but a whole other plant."

The conversation ebbed and flowed through dinner, and afterward, Sam's two sisters, Mel and Daphne, along with Mel's husband, Peter, came to join them.

"You were supposed to sit up at the head table, Lemuel," Daphne said to Sam, giving him a scowl. "We had to put Mr. Harriman and his wife up there to fill the spots."

Lemuel? Chloe mouthed to him, getting a wrinkle of his nose in reply before he answered his sister in the kind of lazy tone brothers know will make their sisters see red.

"It's way more comfortable down here with the plebs," he said, which raised a howl of outrage from almost the entire table.

"Well, you're in for it now anyway," Daphne told him with a smirk. "I heard Mummy telling Aunt Lillian that she's planning to 'have a word' with you..."

Mel giggled. "And we know that one word always leads to many when it comes to our mother."

That led to stories of times gone by, when one or the other of the children—which included Kendrick, Marlon and, later on, Milton—had been caught in one misdemeanor or the other and the consequences thereof. The stories had the entire table, Chloe included, breathless with laughter.

It felt good, she realized, to be in that group. Homey but without the expectations she was so used to having placed on her shoulders. No one looking to her to smooth things over or to take on responsibility for others' lives outside work. She could just be—her.

Even with Sam.

But it was all temporary, and she had to keep reminding herself of that fact. It was no good getting too comfortable, because it was all going to end in a few short weeks.

So when she found Sam's questioning gaze on her face, she just smiled and shook her head, refusing to let any sad thoughts disrupt the lovely evening.

And she kept the tone light on the drive back

home, saying, "I'd forgotten your given name was Lemuel. How on earth did that become Sam?"

He slid her a glance, his lips twitching. "Can you imagine what I went through at school with that name? Luckily for me, most people have never heard it before, and it sounds enough like Samuel for the kids to get confused, so they started calling me Sam, and it stuck."

She giggled. "I think I rather like the name Lemuel. I should start calling you that."

"Don't. You. Dare," he replied, which just made her laugh even harder.

Yet later, when they got back to Sam's place and he set about the comparison between flesh and silk, taking her to new planes of ecstasy in the process, there was, for Chloe, an almost frantic edge to the experience. The need to cram as much passion and intensity into that glorious night so the memory would be indelibly carved into her brain.

Never to fade or be forgotten.

CHAPTER SIXTEEN

CHLOE FELT ALMOST as though she were drifting in a time that bore no resemblance to reality except for when she was in the hospital and actively working. Yet that little corner of her brain, which always insisted good things were never easy, and if they were, never lasted, kept niggling at her.

There was something on Sam's mind, and he wasn't sharing it with her, so she worried at that like a dog with a bone.

More than once she'd found him looking at her with a wrinkled brow or staring off into space in the middle of a conversation. But when she asked him if he wanted to talk, he always smiled and shook his head.

"My mind was wandering," he'd say, going back to whatever he was doing or changing the subject.

She knew there was more to it than he was saying, but didn't try to force the issue.

With no way to know whether what was bothering him had anything to do with her, she found herself falling back into the pattern of taking the blame. It was hard not to, since in the last years of her marriage, she'd taken to walking on egg-shells and trying to actively head off problems that could cause confrontations.

Finn had never been violent, but his rages had been disturbing nonetheless.

Then a phone call from her sister, asking if she was coming home for Christmas, put her in a bad mood.

"Really, Colette? Mum put you up to this, didn't she? I told you all that I'd be home on January first. Why would I fly all the way to London for one day, just to have to fly back and do it all again in a week's time?"

"Stop acting like it's a big deal, Chloe. You can afford it, and it will get Mum off all our backs. She's been ranting about it since you left, until none of us can stand it. You don't work on Christmas Day anyway, so it's completely doable."

For a moment, just one sickening moment, she almost agreed. It was a knee-jerk reaction, brought on by the old ways and the old expectations.

Her entire family assumed she'd bow to their whims and make their lives easier, no matter what it cost her in time, energy or money.

But now she had her baby to think about, and it was time to put a stop to all the nonsense.

"I most certainly will not fly back for Christ-

mas. It's out of the question." When Colette
started arguing, Chloe cut her off. "Listen, I'm
not having a tiff with you about it. You all need
to deal with Mum however you can, but leave
me out of it."

"But it's your fault she's acting up!"

"Well, she needs to get over it. And so do you."

Then, before the call could degenerate into
something worse than it already was, she rang
off.

But the call, coming on the Tuesday morning
as she was getting ready to present a talk to a
gathered group of neurologists invited to Kingston General for that purpose, left her rattled.

Was that what she was facing when she went
home? All the old stressors and demands? Out of
her entire family, the only one she could depend
on for advice was Gran, but to get the advice she
really needed, she'd have to tell the older woman
the entire story.

Was she ready to reveal her pregnancy? Especially to any of her family? Of course, if she
asked Gran not to say anything, she wouldn't, but
it would have to be faced at some point anyway,
so why put it off?

The following morning, she awoke before the
alarm as usual and, instead of getting out of bed,
turned her head to look at Sam, still asleep beside her.

In repose, his face took on an almost stern cast

yet was no less handsome for the lack of mobility, which was what gave him his charm. She could, if she let herself, fall in love with him—more so now than when they'd first met or when they had just started to get to know each other.

Everything he did, even when he was being rather overbearing, seemed aimed at making her comfortable or keeping her and the baby in good health. There were times when she wondered if he was just acting that way because he was on his best behavior, but if it was a charade, it was an exceedingly good one that never faltered.

But he was a force to be reckoned with, both in and out of bed, and no matter how he was presenting himself, she'd seen and been the recipient of the full strength of his character. No amount of mind-blowing lovemaking could make up for being sucked into a relationship and being once more subsumed to her own detriment. It was the last thing on her wish list. Although most everyone else seemed to believe Chloe existed to make them happy or make their lives easier, she was no longer buying what they were selling. For herself, and her child, she could no longer afford it.

Slipping out of bed, she padded downstairs and, after making a cup of tea, fetched her tablet and put in a video call to her gran.

"Hullo darling." Gran's smile was wide, and behind her, the lights of her Christmas tree twinkled. "How are you?"

"I'm good, Gran. And you?"

But Gran didn't answer the question, just narrowed her eyes and said, "You're not all right. I can see it. What's going on?"

Chloe huffed a little laugh. She never could hide from her grandmother.

"Oh, Colette called me yesterday, asking me to fly back for Christmas."

"She lose har mind?" When Gran lost her English accent and fell back into patois, you knew she was upset. "Aren't you coming home in January?"

"Yes. On the first."

Gran kissed her teeth, another sign of great annoyance. "Ridiculous. I hope you told her to go weh."

Chloe chuckled. "Not in so many words, but yes, I told her to go away."

"Good." Gran leaned closer to the camera, as though searching Chloe's face. "And what else?"

It was the moment of truth, and Chloe's heart started thumping so hard, she felt slightly ill.

"Gran, I have something to tell you, and it might be a bit of a shock."

"Go on. Spit it out."

"I'm pregnant."

There was a long pause, during which her grandmother just blinked, her mouth moving but no sound coming out.

Then she said, "Chloe Janice Bailey, tell me

yuh neba tek back dat worthless man yuh did married to!"

Shock had apparently completely shattered Gran's carefully cultivated Britishness, and the evidence of that break made Chloe want to laugh, but she squelched the impulse.

"No, Gran. The baby isn't Finn's. I haven't had anything to do with him since I walked out."

"Thank God. He would have had you in his clutches forever if it was, and I couldn't stand to see that."

Chloe had known her grandmother wasn't overly fond of Finn, but that sounded more emphatic than expected.

"I didn't know you disliked him that much, Gran."

Gran sat back, took off her glasses and rubbed one eye, as though trying to decide what to say. Then her lips firmed, and she said, "Chloe, I watched as Finn stood by and let the family bully you, without doing a thing about it. In fact, he encouraged it, because it gave him an excuse to take advantage of you too. And if you think I didn't notice the way he always made jokes at your expense, acting as though you were the village idiot instead of the capable, competent woman you are, you're mistaken.

"He was bad for you, and your parents and siblings liked him because he allowed them to ride roughshod over you with impunity. I was so glad when you left him, I can't even tell you."

Then, as though the initial statement suddenly struck her again, Gran leaned forward until her nose almost touched the camera.

"But baby girl, the doctors said you couldn't have any children. And if it's not Finn's, whose is it?"

Now for the embarrassing bit, but Chloe wasn't about to back down. Not now. This was a far more pleasant foretaste of what was to come, so she might as well get used to it.

"I met a man at that conference in San Francisco. That's when it happened."

Surprisingly, Gran seemed to take that in her stride. "Does he know about the baby?"

"Yes…" Chloe hesitated for a moment and then decided on full disclosure. "It was the weirdest thing. I came here to Jamaica, and there he was again. So it was easy to tell him, because I didn't have to look far to find him."

Gran's mouth moved, like she was chewing on the words before speaking them, then she gave a decisive nod. "God has a plan for you, that man and the baby you made together. That's why it worked out that way." Then her face fell. "Does that mean you're staying there or planning to move to Jamaica?"

"No, Gran." Why did it hurt so much to say it? It wasn't as though that had ever been a consideration. "I'm coming home as planned. I'm just sort of dreading what the rest of the family will say and how they'll act when they find out."

Gran kissed her teeth again and shook a finger, which would have been in Chloe's face if she'd been there in person. "If I weren't a Christian lady, I'd tell you *exactly* what to tell them if they kick up any fuss."

And Chloe had to laugh, feeling somewhat lighter than she had before and yet somehow sadder at the same time.

Contrarian!

As Chloe said goodbye to her grandmother and switched to checking her email, Sam considered quietly stepping back into the kitchen and pretending he hadn't overheard her conversation. Yet the anger pulsing under his skin wouldn't let him leave well enough alone.

"Chloe…"

She spun around, eyes wide. "Sam. I thought you were still asleep."

He shook his head, fighting for equilibrium. "I woke up when you got out of bed and came down for coffee."

Her eyes narrowed, those storm-cloud lines forming between her brows, and her chin tilted up as it did when she was about to do battle.

"You overheard my conversation."

"Parts of it."

Lips firm, that chin lifting a notch more, she said, "You're angry because I told my grandmother about the baby—"

His hand slashed through the air, cutting her off.

"No, I'm not. The part that made me angry was hearing how your family—and your ex—treated you."

It had been like listening to a story about someone he'd never met, and yet the traces of that old, familiar life had been there.

Having been self-aware enough to recognize the problem, she'd been fighting to throw off those lingering cobwebs. There'd been some times after she first arrived that he'd been caught in the crossfire when she pushed back at his high-handedness, and he hadn't known why.

Instead of mollifying her, he saw her chin go up even higher.

"I'm not that person anymore, so don't get any ideas about bossing me about, now that you know."

Suddenly, his anger waned, and he couldn't help chuckling, as he shook his head.

"You're kidding right?" The lines between her brows deepened, and he hurriedly continued, "It makes me admire you even more. I know how hard it can be to break away from family expectations, and from what I heard, you're doing that in spades."

The lines smoothed out and Chloe nodded.

"It hasn't been easy. When I finally recognized how everyone was manipulating me for their own benefit, I felt like a fool. I'm finished with all that now. I have to do what's right for the baby."

She probably didn't realize it was her loving heart that had made her such a target of her family's selfishness, but Sam did. Walking toward her, he held her gaze, something warm and sweet filling him, so that by the time he was next to her, he couldn't help putting down his cup and tugging her up into his arms.

"You have to do what's right for *you*," he said, reveling in the way she melted against him, resting her cheek against his shoulder and sighing. "Everything else will fall into place."

"I hope so," she replied, her arms around his waist. "But sometimes everything seems so complicated."

That he could understand and agree with, but he didn't want to get into it right then. All he wanted was to hold her and to make her happy. Maybe getting away from everything, including work, would give her a little time to de-stress and gain some clarity?

"I want to take you away next weekend. To Portland, or even Negril, if you're up for it. It'll be nice and quiet, and you'll get to see some of the island. If things were different, I'd say we could go between Christmas and New Year's, but the hospital is always busy and I'll be on call."

"Dr. Owens has set up a two-day conference on December twenty-eight and twenty-nine, as well, so I couldn't go then anyway. He says he wants to get the most out of my time here. But I'd like to do something with you this weekend," she replied, tightening her hold on him for an instant and then easing out of his arms. "Rashida wanted me to go round to their place and help her make Christmas puddings, but I know she can manage without me."

"You don't want to be involved in anything that pint-size sergeant major is doing," Sam replied, the last of his anger draining away when Chloe giggled. "She somehow talked Kendrick, Marlon and me into building her an outdoor brick oven once and wouldn't leave us alone to get on with it. It felt as though she was everywhere at once, issuing orders and making demands."

She was outright laughing now, and Sam realized he'd be quite happy to hear that joyful sound for the rest of his life—a revelation that struck him dumb for an instant.

Then, words rose to his lips, held back only by the knowledge that she wouldn't want to hear them.

Stay. Stay with me.

Worse than knowing she would reject the suggestion out of hand was the knowledge that, somehow, he wasn't even entitled to ask.

CHAPTER SEVENTEEN

RASHIDA REFUSED TO be gainsaid and changed her baking plan from the next weekend to the one after.

"I should have done it from last month," she told Chloe. "I'm already behind times, and if they're not as rum-soaked as some people like it, too bad. I'd rather spend the time with you, enjoying it, than doing it by myself. We'll do steaks on the grill outside—or the men will—and make a party of it."

"I can't remember a busier Christmas than this one," she told Sam, after informing him that the sergeant major had spoken and moved their baking date. "But I haven't done my shopping. In fact, I'd go so far as to say I haven't even thought about it. Have you done yours?"

She was thinking that maybe they could go together, and if she saw anything for him, get Rashida to take her back, but Sam had the nerve to smile a little smugly and say, "Actually, I have. I bought most of my gifts in San Francisco, so

I could get it over with. Besides, then I know no one would get the same thing from someone else."

"Well, you're one up on me. Mind you, I didn't think I'd need to buy gifts this year at all, besides a few souvenirs to take home. Who would have thought I'd have made so many friends while I was here?"

"I don't think anyone would expect you to buy gifts, Chloe."

She shook her head, giving him a smile. "I want to, though. Everyone's been so nice to me, and so welcoming."

It was on the tip of her tongue to say she'd miss them all, but something held her back. Probably the knowledge that she'd miss Sam most of all.

Work was busy that week, and Dr. Owens explained why. "The neurological department is mostly closed between Christmas and New Year's, with each of us taking turns to be on call. There are no clinics or scheduled appointments, which is why I put together that two-day symposium."

"I've contacted my head of department at Royal Kensington and he's sending me some additional information from other research teams, so I hope to make it as interesting as possible. There'll be ample time for Q and A sessions too."

Luckily, her boss had warned her that she'd be expected to do a number of seminars, so she'd come partially prepared. With a bit of work over the next week, she'd get the rest of the information pulled together and be ready to go.

But she was looking forward to her weekend away with Sam. He'd decided to take her to Portland, her grandfather's home parish, and she was excited to go. They planned to leave on Friday afternoon and come back on Sunday, going over Junction Road through the mountains on the way there, and back on the longer route, which went around the coast.

"What time do you think you can be ready to leave this evening?" he asked on Friday morning. "Barring emergency, I'll be done by about four."

"I'm doing a clinic with Dr. Owens this morning and then a presentation to a group of neurological nurse practitioners after lunch. It's slated to finish at three, and then I should be done."

Sam chuckled. "That means you won't be done until four, or haven't you caught the Jamaican vibe yet, where everything goes longer than it should?"

Chloe couldn't help laughing with him. "Very true. I had noticed."

"I'll drive over to the east wing and wait for you outside."

And, as annoying as it was to admit it, Sam was right about the presentation, as she didn't leave the building until four fifteen.

At least Sam had the grace not to say "I told you so."

They'd packed their bags in the car that morning and set out straight from the hospital.

"We have to drive past the house, so we can stop there if you want to change," Sam said, but Chloe just settled back in the seat, prepared to enjoy the drive.

"This is pretty comfortable," she replied. She'd specifically chosen a loose, flowy skirt and cotton shirt and paired them with flats, just for that reason.

Once they left Kingston, the road twisted and turned and climbed up and up into the Blue Mountains. The scenery took Chloe's breath away. Hillsides densely treed would suddenly part, revealing swaths of grassy slopes with stands of bamboo waving feathery arms to the sky. Sam pointed out Castleton Botanical Gardens as they passed, and the name rang a bell.

"I think my granddad mentioned it as somewhere they'd go when he was young, on a Sunday or holiday."

"It was a popular place for day-trippers back in the day. I even remember going there on a school trip once, many, many years ago. What did he say about it?"

"I don't remember," she said with a pang of sadness. "I used to spend quite a lot of time with him when I was young and my grandparents looked after us when we got off from school. Granddad had an old road map that he got in the eighties, which was the last time he was here, and a topographical map, too, and he'd point out some of the places he'd been. He always said that when I got older, we'd come to Jamaica together and see them all."

"Is he still alive?"

"No, unfortunately. He died almost two years ago. He'd had a stroke a few years before and never fully recovered and then had congestive heart failure."

"I'm sorry." He probably recognized the lingering pain in her voice. Sam, she'd noticed, had got surprisingly good at ferreting out her moods, even when she tried to hide them. "And I'm sorry you didn't get a chance to discover the island with him."

"Me, too," she replied. "It would have been a lot of fun. But this trip has been, and continues to be, one of the best I've ever taken, and I'll be remembering him when I see some of the places he talked about."

He murmured agreement, then said, "I finally spoke to Mel, and she told me about your appointment with Ali."

To her ears, he sounded particularly bland, as though the conversation hadn't been a good one.

"Oh?"

"Yes. She was so happy that you seemed to

get it through to Ali that while it's okay to hope that she outgrows her epilepsy, she should still be making plans to mitigate seizures, in case she doesn't."

Relieved that the feedback had been positive, Chloe replied, "I just wanted to be honest with her. Puberty is difficult enough for people without chronic diseases, but in her case, she needs to learn how to calm herself down rather than give in to the temptation to let fly over every little thing. I think she understood what I was trying to say."

"It sounds like she did. She got her mother to enroll her in a yoga class, and Mel says she's taken to it like a duck to water. It's smoothed her out, somewhat."

"Amazing. I'm glad. You know, it'll stand her in good stead, epilepsy or no."

"And give her parents a break too. She was turning into a bit of a brat."

Chloe laughed. "That might have more to do with puberty than anything else. She's pretty much there."

"Don't remind me," Sam groaned. "I can't believe she's twelve already. I swear she was just born. After growing up with two sisters and seeing what's happening with my nieces, I dread the thought of having a daughter."

"Do you?" This was a subject they'd never discussed. "You'd prefer a boy?"

He was silent for an instant and then said, "I just want the baby to be healthy. I don't really care about anything else."

She believed him. There was a strange tone in his voice. One she'd never heard before and couldn't interpret. It made her want to ask him what he was thinking at that moment, but she didn't feel as though she had the right.

This situation was too strange to be demanding confidences or confessions. The only thing she could do was agree but without further comment.

In all, the drive to Port Antonio in Portland Parish took a little over two hours, and it was completely dark when they got to the villa Sam had rented for the trip. Clean and spacious, it was decorated in the colonial style, and Chloe actually gasped when she saw the massive four-poster bed draped with mosquito netting and complete with steps to climb up into it.

"The mattress is higher than my waist," she said, standing beside it for comparison. "I've never seen a bed like this before."

"We'll have to try it out later and see if it's as sturdy as it looks."

That was the start of a glorious couple of days spent swimming, exploring and making love. Sam, as it turned out, had a special affection for Portland, and took Chloe to a number of places, each one more dazzling than the last. Reach Falls and rafting on the Rio Grande were her favorites, although Blue Hole was spectacular and the entire parish, including the sleepy town of Port Antonio, entranced her.

Also during those two nights, Sam seemed more determined than ever to make her crazy with desire. Not that he'd ever failed to satisfy and to leave her love-drunk when it was over, but there was in his touch a different timbre—one that took her to the edge and kept her hovering on the precipice without immediately letting her fly.

It was purposefully done, of course, meant to sharpen need to a razor's edge and intensify the final slash of ecstasy.

But she had her revenge as they made love one last time on Sunday afternoon before embarking on the trip back to Kingston. Taking control, she led him in a slow, erotic dance that promised the pinnacle of release if he could just hold on to his control a little longer. And then a little longer yet.

Once, twice, she almost precipitated the crisis herself, her orgasm springing to the fore almost in full flower, and she had to stop moving so as to regain her equilibrium.

The sound Sam made—pleasure-laden and pleading, both—was almost her undoing, but she wasn't ready to end their journey just yet.

There was a sublime power in looking down at his damp chest and tight face, in feeling the hard grip of his hands on her thighs and the strength of his body beneath hers. It made her light-headed and elated, able to take on anything and everything the world flung her way.

Rocking against him, she gave a soft cry as the perfect angle was achieved, and the hard upthrust of his hips made it sublime. Slowly, with short circles, she started them climbing again, but this time, the ascent was swift, a rocket of sensation and want that was too intense to be denied or forestalled.

She flew straight past the point where she'd meant to halt and shattered around him, shuddering and almost sobbing. Then, before she could get her head back out of the clouds, she was on her back and Sam was above her, his expression ferocious and heartbreakingly beautiful.

She felt his release, the hard pulse of it, but then he was moving with long, hard strokes, somehow causing another rush of sensation that led, amazingly, to another mind-bending orgasm.

And, just then, Chloe knew she'd never have another memory as sweet, both full of promise and yet with that shadow of heartache yet to come.

Three weeks were all that were left, and she was determined to ring every last scintilla of joy and pleasure and *life* out of them.

Lying next to him, satiated and content, she let her mind wander, flitting from subject to subject until it alighted on one she'd been meaning to bring up with him but had let slide before.

"Have you given any thought to baby names?"

She felt him turn his head, as though looking down at where she nestled against his side, but was too languorous to move to meet his gaze.

"Not really," he said softly, with a hesitant note in his voice.

She snuggled closer, putting her leg over his. "You sound surprised I should ask."

"I am, a little," he confessed, his arm tightening around her.

"Well, you shouldn't be. This is your child too."

He didn't reply to that but bent to kiss the top of her head before asking, "Do you have any names picked out?"

"I have a few I like, subject to your approval. I really feel as though this is something we should agree on, you know?"

He stroked her arm and made a little hum of agreement.

"Well, let's hear them."

"For a girl, Adrianna, or Antoinette. I also fancy Olivia and Zara. But I'm really leaning toward my gran's middle name—Victoria."

She felt the change in his body, the way it jerked and then grew stiff, as though zapped with electricity.

"Not Victoria." He didn't sugarcoat it, just flat out refused, and that had Chloe rolling over so as to be able to see his face.

It was ashen, his eyes fierce, and a shiver ran down her spine.

Leave it alone, or ask for an explanation?

The old her would have backed off so as not to upset him more, but the new her, the one who was determined to be strong and forthright, couldn't let it go.

"That's the only name that has any sentimental meaning for me, so I'll need more information before I cross it off the list."

They'd left the mosquito netting open, so there was nothing stopping Sam from rolling over to sit on the edge of the bed, his back to her, stiff and almost preternaturally still.

The silence, broken by only the slow, melodic swish of the overhead fan, seemed to thicken until Chloe felt as though she couldn't breathe.

"It wouldn't be appropriate," he finally said, in a wooden, almost mechanical tone. "That was the name of the woman I planned to marry."

Something inside her shriveled and retreated from his words, but Chloe didn't allow herself to give up.

A voice within was telling her not to react the way she really wanted to, which was to batter him with questions until he was as bruised as she felt. Instead, she kept her voice even, although the effort to do so made her slightly nauseous.

"I guess that's a good reason, especially if she's still in your life."

And might realize through our child's name that you're still in love with her...

Sam got up and walked to the window to stare out for a moment before turning and facing her across the room.

"She died, almost nine years ago." His voice was still flat, but his eyes sparked with so much pain Chloe could hardly bear to keep holding his gaze. "Along with our unborn baby."

CHAPTER EIGHTEEN

SAM WATCHED CHLOE'S FACE, wanting to see her reaction, needing something from her, although he wasn't sure what.

He'd almost convinced himself that he'd never have to tell her about Vicky and the baby. It was, he reasoned, old news. A history that had no bearing on the present. He'd been content— determinedly so—to remain unattached and aloof from romantic ties of any kind. Wallowing, if truth be told, in the old pain. Reluctant to revisit it, in even the remotest sense.

Chloe had mellowed the ache, simply by being herself, and offering him a redemptive chance.

Her eyes were wide, and Sam tried to interpret the emotions he saw flickering in their dark depths, but they were too fleeting.

"I'm sorry, Sam."

She meant it. The sympathy in her voice was unmistakable, yet he also felt as though a new distance yawned between them, and he didn't know why. He'd opened up to her in a way he'd never done before, but instead of it bringing them closer, he thought she was pulling away.

"It was a long time ago, but I'm not going to say the pain went away. In fact, I held on to it and used it as a crutch and a life lesson. I didn't plan to ever marry or have kids. I think what I really wanted was to avoid even the chance of being hurt like that again."

"And my pregnancy being high-risk brought it all back." She nodded, as though she'd reached a decision. "I'm sorry for that."

"Don't be." Sam felt suddenly on shaky ground. The weekend had been so wonderful, but now he felt everything slipping away. "You weren't to know. And it's not like any of this was planned."

"No." Chloe slipped from the bed and headed for the bathroom. "You're right about that, but I would have been more sensitive about the name issue if I'd known about your ex beforehand." Sam took a step toward her, although he didn't have a clue what he was going to say, but she paused in the doorway and looked back. When he saw the lines between her brows, his heart sank even further. "Not that it's any of my business, mind you," she continued, giving him a smile that didn't quite reach her eyes, before stepping into the bathroom and closing the door.

Shutting him out.

Suddenly angry, he let her go and set about getting dressed.

He'd bared his pain to her , and she'd walked away. If she wanted to be unreasonable instead of talking things out, then there was nothing he could do about it except wait and let her cool down.

It wasn't as if she'd been terribly forthcoming with him about her past either. Oh, she'd told him she was divorced and that it was because her ex had cheated on her repeatedly, but only when he'd heard her conversation with her grandmother had he learned the whole truth.

He heard her come out of the bathroom as he was pulling on his shirt and couldn't resist glancing her way as she rummaged in her bag for some clothes.

Even in profile he could see her lips were tight, and he was sure those lines would be back between her eyes. His anger bled away, leaving him mentally scrabbling for a way to make things right.

"Listen, I'm sorry I never mentioned it before, but I honestly didn't think it had anything to do with our situation. With us."

Her head tilted slightly, as though she was considering his words, and then she nodded.

"Sure, I can see why you'd think that."

"What does that mean, exactly?"

He had to pin her down, make sure they weren't talking at cross-purposes.

She turned then to face him, and her expression made his heart stutter. It wasn't angry, or upset, but blank. Closed to him in a way he'd never seen before.

And she shrugged, the movement casually dismissive.

"The reality is, that besides our baby, we have nothing. We agreed to have a bit of fun while we were figuring the rest of it out, so no—your prior relationships really are none of my business."

For a moment he couldn't speak, the sting of her words raising a rush of prickling heat over his skin.

"Do you really classify what's happened between us as *nothing*?"

The corners of her lips tipped up in an ironic, hurtful little smile.

"Well, the sex has been terrific," she said, and there was amusement in her voice. "But, seriously, we knew going in that it was just a crazy coincidence that brought us together and we'd be going our separate ways in short order."

"But…"

Sam faltered, the words he'd been about to say sticking in his throat.

He'd been about to tell her that he wanted her to stay in Jamaica. Maybe even confess that he'd thought about marriage and them making a home together, here or in England, but she'd just said there was nothing of substance between them. So why even bother?

"Exactly," Chloe said, that slightly mocking smile still on her face, her eyes dark and unfathomable. "Come on, let's get on the road. You said you wanted to get back to Kingston before nightfall."

And with that, the conversation was apparently over.

It was only when they got close to the city, after an almost silent drive, that he realized the worst of the fallout was yet to come.

"I'm going to stay at the apartment," Chloe said, her tone conversational, as though it didn't much matter what he thought. "I just need to get some clothes for work and I'll grab a taxi."

He wanted to tell her no. To say that wasn't what he wanted—wasn't what was right for them. Maybe even play on that sweet, conciliatory side of hers to get what he desired. Anger rose, luckily choking him before any of the words were said, and he inhaled a long, deep breath, fighting for control.

"Sure," was what he finally got out, past what felt like barbed wire in his throat. "But I'll drop you off when you're ready."

And it was only after he'd done just that, and watched her walk into the apartment building, that he realized the choking sensation wasn't born of anger.

But of fear.

She'd known what she was getting into with Sam Powell. She'd been warned and had even said it herself. He was her last chance at a no-strings-attached fling. One without everlasting commitment or complication.

But, standing in her Christmas-denuded flat, Chloe realized she hadn't listened.

Not to Rashida nor to herself.

Instead of keeping her baby's father at an emotional arm's length, she'd dropped her guard and fallen for him—hard.

It was, she knew, all on her. Yes, she was hurt and upset with Sam for not telling her about losing his ex-girlfriend and their baby, but if she'd stuck to the original plan, it wouldn't have been so painful.

Now she could understand all too well his reluctance to become involved with another woman. And it was just as well he'd made that choice, because no one could compete with a ghost.

Chloe wouldn't even try.

She'd been a willing—if somewhat unwitting—doormat in her previous relationship. There was no way she'd be a poor replacement for a deceased woman in her next.

And now she also understood Sam's obvious worry about her pregnancy and both his willingness to accept that he was about to become a father as well as his concern for her well-being. It had all been out of fear of losing another child.

What Chloe had seen as evidence of his growing care for her, personally, and a developing relationship had been born out of that fear.

His feelings for her—beyond the sexual attraction—were strictly because she was the receptacle for the life she carried in her womb.

Going out onto the balcony, Chloe came to the realization that for the baby's sake, not to mention her own, some hard decisions had to be made.

What she wanted was to walk away completely, leaving Sam—and hopefully this heartache—behind, but that wasn't possible. He was still the father of her child, and some contact with him was inevitable. She just couldn't handle it right now when she was raw and heartsore, with every nerve exposed.

Tears made her neighbors' twinkling lights shimmer, as though mocking her misery, reminding her what she'd just lost.

Even if it had just been an illusion, she'd been so happy living it. More content than she could ever remember being in her life. Now she had to face the fact that it was over.

Forever.

Using the tips of her fingers to wipe away the

moisture from her eyes, she straightened her back and tried to find the elusive silver lining she knew had to be there somewhere.

Falling back on the benefits she'd thought of after her divorce—her job and freedom to do whatever she wanted—didn't bring the joy they had before. But that was what she had. At least until the baby was born.

Cupping her palms over the slight bump of her stomach, she whispered, "We'll be okay."

Saying it more to herself than to the baby.

She didn't expect Sam to call her over the next couple of days, but he did, and she didn't answer. After the second time, he sent her a text, telling her to phone him when she was ready to talk.

That made her snort. If he left it at that, he might never hear from her again. While she was able to hold it all together at work, despite constantly looking over her shoulder in case Sam was around, just the thought of talking to him made tears flood her eyes.

She really had to get herself together before that particular conversation.

Not feeling up to socializing or explaining to Rashida what was happening, Chloe sent her friend a text on Monday morning, saying she was working on her presentation for the next few days. The person she really wanted to talk to was Cora, but from the sounds of it, her friend was having her own problems, and Chloe didn't want to burden her with anything else.

On top of it all, there was the growing sense that she needed to handle this all herself, as a testament to her inner strength. She didn't *need* Sam or anyone else to make it through life, she reminded herself stoutly, even though the thought brought with it a hard pang of sadness.

Getting ready for bed after three days of hard thinking, she came to a decision.

The following day she'd call Sam and arrange a meeting with him. She needed to get the rest of her clothes from his house anyway, and it was a good excuse to sit down and talk this all out.

At some point, before she left, they'd have to get everything settled, and the anticipation of that conversation was causing even more stress than just having it and being done would.

Settling under the sheet, Chloe pulled up the information her colleague in London had sent regarding neurofibromatosis research and started reading through. Although she'd used getting prepped for the seminar as an excuse to avoid company, she was well pleased with the amount of work she'd actually been able to do.

And before long, she felt sleep creeping up on her and turned out the light, somehow more serene than she'd been for days. Making up her mind about how to deal with Sam had lifted a weight off her spirit.

When she awoke, it was to darkness and a sensation both familiar and unwelcome.

Back pain, excruciating and unrelenting, bad enough that she held her breath, too afraid to even exhale, in case it got worse.

Still trapped in a somnolent state, she recognized it as the start of her period and tried to remember where she'd left her pills.

Then the rush of awareness, the fear—more potent and grinding than the pain itself—had her reaching for her phone on the bedside table.

Mindless with terror, she didn't even think, just pushed the button.

When Sam answered, all she could do was gasp, "Call Dr. Hall. I have to go to the hospital."

CHAPTER NINETEEN

SAM PUT HIS hand on Chloe's shoulder, needing to feel her warmth under his palm, but there was little sensation in his fingers.

Millicent Hall was speaking, and he forced himself to listen.

"It really is an old wives' tale that pregnancy is a good way to get rid of endometriosis. While some women get some relief from the symptoms during pregnancy, others don't."

She looked down at the chart in her hand, flipping a page back and then forth again.

Sam wanted to shout at her to hurry up, to tell them whatever the hell she had to say.

Chloe shifted, and the brief touch of her cheek against his fingers steadied him slightly and made him realize his grip on her was probably too tight.

He loosened his fingers.

"All the tests have come back negative. There is no bleeding and the ultrasound showed no abnormalities or masses. Chloe's temperature is within normal range, so I'm tentatively confident there's no infection."

He must look even worse than he felt, Sam thought, because Millie was speaking to them as though they were ordinary people instead of doctors.

No bleeding, instead of "spontaneous abortion."

No abnormalities or masses rather than "hemoperitoneum" or "endometriomas."

Not "sepsis caused by intestinal perforations or changes in endometriotic lesions due to decidualization," but just plain old *infection.*

She didn't say the words, but she didn't have to, because Sam's brain supplied them itself, running through all the possible permutations until he thought he'd go bonkers.

Damn him for researching the condition and its possible effects on the pregnancy, once he knew Chloe had it. A little ignorance would be bliss just now.

"I think what we're seeing is simply a manifestation of Chloe's underlying condition. A continuation of her symptoms rather than a clear-and-present danger to her pregnancy. Endometriosis during pregnancy can almost be distilled into a battle of hormones. If the progesterone wins, there's a relief from symptoms. If the estrogen wins, there isn't. Tonight, the estrogen was stronger."

"Can I go home?" Chloe's voice was faint, far-away, but knowing she didn't mean his house made him, ridiculously, want to weep.

"I'm going to keep you in," Millie said. "To monitor your condition overnight. But if all goes well, you'll be discharged in the morning."

Then with a nod, she left.

Sam was rooted where he stood. The adrenaline surge he'd felt when Chloe woke him up had waned, leaving him cold and shaken. He couldn't even remember the drive from his house to the hospital. Knowing he wasn't in the best of conditions to drive, he'd arranged for an ambulance to pick Chloe up, but he'd arrived at the same time and hadn't left her side since.

Chloe put her hand up and her fingers were as icy as Sam's.

"Why don't you go home?" she said. "And get some rest. I'll be okay."

Did she really want—*expect*—him to leave?

Should he ask or just take it as a given that she wanted to be alone?

A nurse bustled in at that moment and gave them a smile, as though the bottom hadn't dropped out of his *rass* life and been carried away by gut-tearing fear.

"Doctor said I'm to give you something to help you sleep."

"See," Chloe said, her voice strangely calm, yet she sounded almost as numb as Sam felt inside.

"There's nothing more you can do here, Sam. Go home."

He bent, meaning to kiss her cheek, but found himself resting his forehead on her hair, his fingers still gripping her shoulder, reluctant to let go.

"Sleep well," he finally said, aware of the nurse watching them and the sympathy in her eyes.

With a soft kiss on her cheek, he left the room and stood outside the door, unable to get his feet to go a step farther.

Millie had met them at Andrews Memorial, a hospital Sam knew well, but which now seemed as unfamiliar as the shadow world of a dream. Objectively, he knew he was suffering from shock or, at the very least, the tail end of the adrenaline dump, but he couldn't seem to figure out how to treat it.

Physician, heal thyself.

The old saying rose in his brain and drifted away again.

"Dr. Powell?" He turned at the sound of his name to see another nurse coming toward him. "Dr. Hall said to tell you that there's an empty private room just down the hall, if you want to stay and need to lie down."

"Thank you," he said automatically, but instead of following her pointed finger, he wandered down the corridor and, taking a back route, went outside, behind the main building.

The night was cool, but Sam was already shivering before he got out the door, so a little night breeze meant nothing. Walking along the edge of the carpark, he found a spot behind a tree where the streetlights couldn't reach and sank down onto the ground.

The look on Chloe's face when he'd rushed to the stretcher, the stark terror in her eyes would stay with him forever.

He'd known then that she thought she was losing the baby, and her fear had infected him like a superbug, bringing with it all the grief and agony he'd endured before.

Even now, his hands shook and his entire body felt like jelly,

And yet he had to remind himself, the worst had not happened. The pain and terror would pass, and they still had a chance to...

To what? What do you want, Sam?

The moment of truth was upon him, and he knew it but couldn't corral his faculties enough to think it through.

Every nerve and sinew in his body strained to go back inside and be with Chloe. To protect her with life and limb and whatever else he had to bring to bear.

He hadn't wanted a child. Had even less wanted to feel the way he did about Chloe, but this wasn't a choice anymore.

It was all there, lying in that hospital bed, and

although he knew full well none of it was his for the taking, he wanted it—them—nonetheless.

Chloe had filled a hole in his heart, and in his life, that he'd hardly dared to admit even existed. Looking back, he'd kept busy with work and all the extracurricular activities a man could ever want, but when he went home at night, there'd been no joy, no meaning to any of it.

The weeks with Chloe—weeks of fear and fun and infuriation—had meant more to him than the last ten years of his life.

When Vicky died, he'd felt cheated—not only out of being a parent but out of all the little steps leading up to it too.

The excitement of hearing they were going to have a child.

The first trip to the doctor and the plans for the future—everything from choosing names and nursery colors to where would be the best place to raise the baby.

The first sonogram, where they could see the new life in its very beginning stage.

Vicky had, for whatever reason, deprived him of all of it, and he'd resented her for doing that.

Chloe had had every opportunity to do the same but hadn't.

She'd told him about the baby as soon as she'd known herself and allowed him into Millie's office, when she could very well have asked him to stay in the waiting room. Allowed him that first glimpse of the life they'd created together.

She'd even wanted to consult with him on the name.

Everything he'd been deprived of before she'd lovingly given of her own accord.

And given of herself too.

Not just her body, but her sweet, practical, loving spirit too.

She was one in a billion.

A hundred billion.

His first impulse was to go in there and snatch at it, make demands and issue ultimatums. But he knew that wouldn't work, and even if it did, it wouldn't last.

The one thing he wanted most of all was the one thing he didn't think she'd be willing to give.

Her heart.

Hospitals are no place to get well.

As she drifted up from her blessedly drugged sleep, Chloe found herself wondering who'd first said that, even as she acknowledged the truth of it. How difficult it was to consider getting better when there was always some type of racket going on.

For the patient who simply craved peace and a quiet place to think, the wards—even a private room—in a hospital were the worst possible place to be.

Lying on her side, she could see the window where a thin stream of murky light came through the blinds to one side. Weak sunlight, she thought, rather than streetlamps with their harsh glare.

She knew where she was. The sounds of a hospital in the morning were nothing new. What *was* new was this feeling of utter impotence, of rage, that her body—even having been given this precious gift—continued on its path of betrayal and fearmongering.

Sam's face.

She could hardly bear to think about his expression, the absolute agony she'd seen in those moments when he'd run to her side. Thinking, no doubt, about those he'd lost before, terrified their child would be added to the tally.

He'd rallied, of course. He was used to emergencies and knew how to put his own fear aside so as to give the support she'd needed.

That was the kind of man any woman would be proud to have beside her—one who would always have her back, no matter what.

The man she would love for the rest of her days.

"You're awake."

His voice had her closing her eyes, not to pretend sleep but to battle back the tears she'd been about to shed.

When she rolled over, he was there to reposition her pillows and pull up the sheet, his hands tender and careful.

She lifted her chin, facing him, looking straight into his face for the first time since he'd spoken.

He looked pale. His eyes were red, as though he hadn't slept.

"Did you get any sleep last night?"

He gestured to the chair beside her bed.

"It wasn't terribly comfortable, so no."

Her silly heart leaped with the knowledge that he'd stayed, but she forced it to calm.

"You should have gone home. There was nothing you could do here."

The look he gave her was long and searching, then he shrugged.

"On the contrary, there was a lot I could do. I watched you sleep and made sure that if the pain woke you up, I'd be here to get you the help you'd need."

"That's what the nurses are for." It was hard to dismiss his words, but Chloe knew she had to. This thing between them couldn't go on. Not like this.

Not when it hurt both of them so much. The last thing she wanted was to add to his pain.

He shook his head and looked as though he would perch on the side of her bed, then thought better of it. Instead, he brought the chair closer and sat down.

"No, that's what I was for last night." Before

she could speak in response, he continued. "I know all too well what it really means not to be able to do anything at all for someone you care about, and that wasn't the case last night."

He cared about her.

Again her silly heart leaped, and again she subdued it. Of course he cared. For the baby, perhaps even for her, as a friend, a lover. Nothing more.

"I didn't tell you the entire story about Vicky, and I need to, so you'll understand."

He paused, but didn't look away, keeping his dark, pain-filled gaze on her until Chloe was sure her heart would break. Something told her she didn't want to hear any more, and she should stop him from telling it, but no words could pass the tightness of her throat. Instead, she nodded, knotting her fingers into the sheets so as not to reach out and try to smooth away the lines around his eyes.

"She died in a car crash and…" Now he hesitated, and she saw him swallow. "It was only when she was gone that I found out she was pregnant. Four months pregnant."

"Sam—"

Words failed her, even as questions rushed through her brain and a cold, sinking feeling settled in her stomach. He'd not only lost the woman he'd loved but she'd betrayed his trust too.

How could he ever get over that?

She saw it now, the final blow poised above her

head, but Chloe refused to bow before it. Hadn't she, oh-so-stupidly, told herself she could handle whatever came her way? Well, this was the chance to put her money where her mouth was and keep her dignity.

"You don't have to say any more, Sam. I understand."

He cocked his head, and his eyes narrowed. "Do you?"

"Yes." How ridiculous to be proud of the firmness of her voice, when inside she was already wailing. "I don't want you to be hurt again either. Before you know it, I'll be flying back to England and out of your hair."

He got up so abruptly the chair scraped across the floor, and he scrubbed his hand across his jaw, as though trying to take off the skin.

"If that's what you think—" He broke off, and cursed under his breath. Then he inhaled, and said, "If that's what you want."

"I do." There, it was done. Over with. If the blasted man would just leave so she could cry in peace, she'd be okay.

"Chloe…"

"Just go, Sam. Don't make it harder than it needs to be."

"Harder? For whom?"

The spurt of anger was welcome and Chloe embraced it.

"For you. For me. For all of us. If you need to

leave, then go. Don't let some ridiculous sense of responsibility keep you here."

He was beside the bed, but she couldn't see him because she was crying. Angry with herself, and with him, for reducing her to this state of weakness.

"I don't feel responsible for you, Chloe." His tone was hard, and it hurt enough that she dashed away her tears so as to glare at him as he continued, "You're a grown woman, competent and smart. You can, and have, taken responsibility for yourself. Why should I try to take that away from you? But what I do feel is love, and I don't want to go."

He hadn't said *love*, had he? Not with that stern, forbidding expression on his face?

"Wh-what?"

"I love you, Chloe. And I love the baby you're carrying, and I don't want to go, and I don't want you to go back to England either. What I want is to be with you, through the good or bad. Life isn't easy, but you make everything in my life better, and I want that to continue, forever."

She knew she was gaping at him like a fool while the blood rushed and bubbled in her veins, like champagne.

"I'll only go if you tell me there's no chance in hell that you would ever love me back, because if there's even the slightest hint—"

"I love you too."

The words slipped out and couldn't be recalled even if she wanted to do such a thing. Sam pulled her into his arms and kissed her until her head swam, and she knew she'd never be whole without him again.

"Oy!" The nurse sounded as though she couldn't decide whether to be angry or amused. "None of that, you two. This is a respectable place, not a motel."

And Chloe could only bury her heated face in Sam's chest and laugh her joy aloud.

EPILOGUE

Zara Lucinda Powell made her way into the world, via scheduled cesarean section on a hot, humid night in June and came out wailing as though completely over the entire experience already.

"Beautiful," Millie Hall said, as she laid Zara on Chloe's chest and Sam cut the cord. "Nothing wrong with her Apgar score, I'm sure."

Still dazed, Chloe looked down at the perfect little being, murmuring encouragement, relieved beyond words that, even with everything that had happened, this moment had finally arrived.

Not endometriosis nor placenta previa, which had caused the C-section, could dim the joy.

Zara stilled, looking up into her mother's face, and Chloe got a thrill of pleasure when she realized their baby had Sam's eyes.

"She's perfect," Sam said, and the wonder in his voice matched her own. When he reached out a finger and smoothed it across the baby's head,

Chloe fought back tears. "Perfect, just like her mother."

"Mama, can I take her for a minute? I'll bring her right back," the nurse said, smiling and holding out her hands—asking but really telling, in that way good nurses know how to do.

When the nurse whisked their once-more screaming offspring away to weigh her and give her a quick cleaning, Sam reached down and rested his cheek on Chloe's head.

"Good job, Mrs. Powell," he whispered into her ear. "You came through like a champ."

She snorted. "All I had to do was lie here. Millie did all the work."

Dr. Hall looked over the drape and laughed behind her mask. "Tell me that two days from now when the incision site makes it hard to even cough."

But even that couldn't stop Chloe from grinning behind her surgical mask.

How could she not be happy?

She and Sam had been married on Boxing Day in Kendrick and Rashida's garden, and their life together so far had been magical. Chloe, after long discussions with Sam, had decided that living in Jamaica would be best for them all and had taken a post at University Hospital, where she was also lecturing.

And now, their sweet little girl had finally arrived.

"It's worth it," she said, smiling up at Sam, who was watching what the nurse was doing with Zara and didn't notice. "It's definitely all been worth it."

He looked down at her then, and they shared one of those looks that always made her melt.

"Yes," he agreed softly. "Every minute worth it, for all this."

* * * * *

Look out for the next story in
The Christmas Project quartet

December Reunion in Central Park
by Deanne Anders

And there are two more
Christmas stories to come
Available December 2021!

If you enjoyed this story, check out these
other great reads from Ann McIntosh

Island Fling with the Surgeon
Night Shifts with the Miami Doc

All available now!